THE HOUSE OF MATHILDE

THE HOUSE OF MATHILDE

HASSAN DAOUD

Translated from the Arabic by
Peter Theroux

Granta Books
London

Granta Publications, 2/3 Hanover Yard, London N1 8BE

Originally published under the title of *Binâyat Mathilde*
by Dâr al-Tanwîr, Beirut, 1983
First published in Great Britain by Granta Books 1999

A CIP catalogue record for this book
is available from the British Library.

1 3 5 7 9 10 8 6 4 2

Typeset by M Rules
Printed and bound in Great Britain by
Mackays of Chatham PLC

THE HOUSE OF MATHILDE

Part One

My aunt was alone in the building. No one stood at the large windows that lighted the stairs and separated the floors. No one opened their door. It seemed to me that the doors had been locked for a long time. They were imposing and silent, and the big iron padlocks that dangled from them suggested that the old furniture within had long been shrouded in darkness. Anyone who had known Mathilde could imagine the thick dust that covered the sofas, beds, and wooden tables.

There was no one in the building, or so I thought; I felt the emptiness as I stood on my aunt's rear balcony. The other balconies were empty, and the fine white tiles with which

Madame Laure had paved her cement balcony looked dusty and old. The wind had piled leaves, dirt and fine sand in its corners and edges. Madame Laure's door was closed. I knew I would not hear the sound of her frying pan suddenly sizzling and then dying down. I would not see her clean kitchen apron. My aunt would not wait patiently for the stream of questions the Armenian woman used to ask her.

My aunt was alone in the building. She feared the cold of the sunny winter days, and so she always walked quickly from the kitchen out on to the balcony. She almost ran, her ample buttocks shaking, though her movements were ponderous. She had aged. You could tell that from the way she wore her many layers of woollies, her rumpled ankle socks, the way she closed the door when she went back into the kitchen from the balcony.

The cold of the sunny winter day fell on her cheeks and left mild panic in her eyes as she looked at me. The cold penetrated her heavy haunches, her woollen stockings and thick clothing. It penetrated the wall that separated the adjacent balconies, with the wide water pipes and disintegrating timbers of the kitchen and bathroom windows. The cold sun fell on the yellow wall, restoring it to its past brightness; on the rotten wooden frame of the bathroom window, recalling a time when it was clean and strong. The building was no longer habitable. It was good only for its old tenants to gather on one of its balconies when they visited. They would speak little, laugh and shout, and then go back home to their new flats.

No one who had left the building ever came back to live in it. My aunt was alone in the building. As always, she would still put full plates of food on the kitchen table. She still did her own laundry, holding up the shirts and shaking them in the air, scattering a cold spray of tiny drops of water on her hands and face. Briskly she would hang out the laundry on the line, then step inside, where she kept all her kitchen things.

As if the cold of the winter sun affected only her. She shivered exaggeratedly, then called for me to sit anywhere but in the kitchen, as if trying to give the impression that there were many rooms, many places to sit. My aunt's apartment nullified my visits, no matter how often I came to see her; whenever I entered it, it was as though I was visiting her for the first time – as if I were opening the doors for the first time after a long absence.

The building was no longer habitable. The dim grey steps were soft and hollowed out from the hard tramping of so many feet. The black iron handrail was scratched, and its corners were no longer sharp; the angles indistinct. Its surface looked wet, as though the sweat of all the palms that had brushed it had sunk into it. The iron of the railing was no longer as steady as it had been. The edges of the stone steps were worn, and some had fallen out of place, especially from the upper steps. Not only the steps, but the small balconies which were cut from the same stone as the stairs, and surrounded by the same black railing, looked fragile in the sunny winter light.

Madame Gadijian had discovered that the building was no longer habitable a long time ago. Her daughters refused to let the porters carry their luggage down. They themselves brought down the leather suitcases, big parcels, books, paintings from the fifth floor. They were delighted with their new house. Madame Gadijian left the building lightly, easily, as if she was going out to visit someone and was coming right back. Her husband carried the large copper pot with a sort of sharp axe embossed at its centre. Madame Gadijian told my aunt one day, when I was too young to understand the meaning of what she said, that the pot and the axe were the emblem of Armenia, a country which she had left, never to return.

The faucet in the Western-style bathroom belonged to an era when artisans invested even the smallest utilitarian things with splendour. With its several rings and different widths of spout, it was like something from the pillars of an old citadel. I turned on the faucet, and the water gushed out just as it did many years ago. It rushed out, cold and clear. I looked out of the bathroom window at the wall of the building opposite. It was so close. That was the way it was, and it had not changed. I looked down at the narrow alley that separated our building from the block of flats opposite.

Madame Gadijian only once came back to the building. Immediately after the departure of her old neighbour, Madame Laure started talking about the spaciousness of the new house and the way the new tiles gleamed. It was not far away, she said, but Madame Gadijian's husband was paying such an exorbitant rent that no one in their building could even imagine it. Madame Laure said that her old neighbour had told her how her daughter Alice was doing. She was no longer afraid of that mysterious thing that used to make her feel for her skirt all the time, as if afraid of someone suddenly appearing out of nowhere and pulling it down.

Alice's legs were white. No one could imagine their whiteness who had not seen her fine black hair: it was short, and shook whenever she moved her head, cut high at the back over her tall and slender neck.

My aunt had changed nothing in the Western-style bathroom. The faucets themselves had not changed. The colour of the marble floor had not faded. Once I burned my hand on the heater underneath the water tank. I can still see the mark the burn made, where the small red-hot furnace window touched it. The bathroom was as it had always been; nothing had changed. My aunt's husband still put his shaving things on the ledge of the mirror above the sink. I picked up the tube of cream and dabbed some on my chin, and in the old mirror the foam began to appear, only one patch in the middle of the glass still actually reflecting.

The bathroom was always immersed in brilliant light. The water would gush copiously out of the high shower, and steam rise from my small body. The busy sounds from the rooms and hallways reached the warm, well-lit bathroom, even under the shower, as if the bathroom were placed right in the midst of all the clamour. Our cleanliness used to make all of us freshly bathed children enjoy strolling from room to room, exuding fragrance, our shining faces diffused among the mirrors, tiles, and beds.

But my aunt changed the colours of the walls and ceilings after we left. The whole flat seemed to expand around her. She locked the doors leading to the large sitting room and dining room after furnishing them with sofas, chairs, and a new table. She also put a large landscape painting on the wall opposite the main sitting-room door. She made no further changes in the dining-room furniture, and the salon furniture stayed the way she had arranged it. She stopped thinking about it for as long as the doors were locked.

Now I stood before the hidden rooms, turned the knob, and pushed the door slowly. A sofa appeared, lurking in the dim light. Habib told me that his father sent for him to come to Venezuela. He was brown-skinned and lazy, and spoke very slowly; he said that he would travel there with his mother and sister. He seemed grown up to me as he stood in his thick-striped pyjamas, in the middle of the room that my aunt later turned into a locked dining room.

I used to sleep in the corner of the room, near the door that led to the little balcony. The room was brighter than it was now – warmer and more spacious. Habib paced constantly between the doors. After his father's departure, he did not have to wait long. He left with his mother, just like that, in a fleeting moment, as if the plane had passed over the building and snatched him from the roof.

Umm Habib, his mother, left nothing that would have indicated they had ever lived in the flat. She took even the large armoire, which I thought would be impossible to fit through the door and transport to her brother's distant house. There she stored everything in a room and locked the door, to await her return from Venezuela with her husband.

The departure of Umm Habib and her children made the flat a little roomier. My aunt and mother reassigned the rooms between them. At the time I did not wonder why they didn't apportion the flat on the basis of adjoining rooms. We got the front room and the one right at the back. Our sofas, upholstered in dark burgundy with polished wooden sides, were in the salon beside my aunt's sofas and her small tea tables.

When I opened the door to the little balcony, I saw the winter sun giving colour to the tops of buildings separated from ours by the long, wide park. I had never seen this view before. I had never opened the door giving on to the buildings that stood beyond the park. On opening it, I looked closely at the railing and at the surface of the balcony; I gazed at the quiet street and at the people heading for the park.

The adjoining balcony, the apartment's second balcony, whose door opened on to the next room, was always empty. No one ever stood there. The neighbours' second balcony was always empty too. I remember that at the al-Kilanis' flat down on the second floor, they all crowded on to the one balcony every evening, while the adjacent balcony lay empty, as if it were not part of their flat.

My aunt, trembling from the cold, and no longer embarrassed to wear woollen ankle socks, abandoned the whole flat and lived in the kitchen and the room next to it. She fixed up a place in the room for sitting and napping, and for receiving visiting relatives. She could not be bothered to fill it with the right furniture; it was enough for her that her visitors knew that she had proper furniture in the locked salon and dining room. Several chairs were set along the sides of her sitting room. They were old and sagging, upholstered in fabric decorated with small, pale flowers. My aunt was very attentive to cleanliness; otherwise she would not have continued to lug out the blue plastic bucket and hang her wet and damp clothing along the laundry line that stretched from one end of the balcony to the other.

Abu Ibrahim al-Kilani died a natural death. He simply did not wake up when his wife tried to rouse him. She shook him a few times, but he lay stretched out like a board. Then she knew. She began to cry, softly at first, then more loudly, her voice rising, mounting through the building, until my aunt heard it up on the fifth floor and said that someone had died in the al-Kilanis' flat.

Umm Ibrahim's cries were soon joined by others. The weeping was continuous and pitched in a single insistent tone. I eavesdropped from the open window, imagining that the women were crying while still going about their household work. Abu Ibrahim's sister, for example, was crying with her eyes wide open, as if counting how many mourners had arrived to offer condolences. Umm Ibrahim was carrying the bedding around in her hands, and piling it up. She was putting it away with the folded sheets, and looking around, looking for some other chore to do, without a pause in her continuous, monotonous sobbing.

I imagined the clamour and crying rising from the room three floors beneath mine, and the pile of mattresses to which Umm Ibrahim was adding one in the same place where my mother piled our bedding. The room near the kitchen, leading to their large rear balcony, was the same as in our flat. Even the furniture in the two rooms was set out in almost the same way. The bedding was in one corner, the table with the radio on it in another, and a coffee table and a shabby sofa in the middle.

The al-Kilanis' flat was the only one in the building whose interior I could visualize. I could accurately describe the large doors of the bedroom closet. I could also see the swollen wooden sides of the sofas, and the colour of the sofas, too. The al-Kilanis had added little to speak of to their huge unadorned pieces of furniture, of the kind which I had seen in my relatives' flats. They had not changed anything in the arrangement and placement of the furniture, to the point that their flat, which I had never entered, became familiar to me, and I reckoned that I could have walked around in it without embarrassment or hesitation.

Sometimes, however, especially when I saw Umm Ibrahim al-Kilani, her children, and her mother-in-law on the balcony facing the park, I figured that they must have some unusual wooden ornaments on their furniture, something distinct about the type of furnishing inherited by the al-Kilanis and which they moved from place to place. These wooden pieces would be elongated, perhaps, and painted on one side; I had seen them in my mind's eye, but had never once succeeded in locating one of them on a table, shelf, or window sill. I found no match anywhere for this strange additional furniture, but knew it would be there, carefully wrapped in old cloth and hidden in one of their large wardrobes.

Every afternoon, Umm Ibrahim, her children, and her mother-in-law squeezed on to one of the two parallel balconies that overlooked the park. They crowded on to one balcony and left the other completely empty. There was no room for the children to play on the balcony, or even to move around. They sat, like their mother and grandmother, without seeming ever to get irritated or bored. They gazed at the spacious park, and every so often one of them stood up and raised his head over the black railing, to look down into the street that separated the building from the park.

The children obeyed their mother, otherwise they would not have been able to stay out on the balcony with her every afternoon. Ibrahim only left the flat to go to school, and Fawzia, who suffered from chronic inflammation of her tonsils, looked, despite her slender build, like her mother. Her voice was like her mother's too, and so was her hair, which was chestnut-coloured, almost blonde. Even Fawzia's slim feet somehow resembled her mother's plump lower limbs. Fawzia was growing up to look so much like her that I was positive that the mother kept all her old clothes so that Fawzia could eventually wear them.

Umm Ibrahim could be seen outside the door of her second-floor flat, her dress soaked with water. She would be washing the door and its glass pane, lifting the mouth of the jug as high as she could. Against the door, her white complexion looked dull and her large mouth revealed a set of teeth that seemed to indicate her simplemindedness. She stopped me on the stairs and asked about my mother and aunt. She looked like her daughter Fawzia, and like my mother too, as if she were a relative, or someone from my mother's parents' quarter of the village in the South.

The al-Kilanis were always seen either on the balcony, where they sat in rows, as if they were sitting in a long car, or at the door as if one of them was getting ready to leave. No one ever saw Abu Ibrahim the father. Once I saw him from behind; I was unable to imagine what his face looked like. He was rather short, and I thought of him as working in a shoe factory: placing the leather on the wooden last and pulling it down tight on the sides, down to the heel of the last.

He walked with his head bowed, his arms unmoving. He always walked that way, said my father. My father also said that Abu Ibrahim was the only person who never greeted anyone he met on the stairs, as if he lived in some other building.

Because of what was said about Abu Ibrahim, I began to think he was younger than the men who were so generous with greetings on the stairs. He did not seem like a father of children, and I began to think that he did not talk to his children at home. He only talked to Umm Ibrahim, who looked after him. She set out his food on the little table in their living room. He ate with his face turned to the wall. When he was finished eating, he got up with both his hands raised, as if bearing them to the sink, afraid of bumping into something.

Abu Ibrahim was the first person in the building to die. He ate and then went to the sink holding his hands out. He washed them, went to bed, and never woke up.

None of the family's habits changed after he died. They continued to sit out on the little balcony, and kept to their accustomed places. Ibrahim and Fawzia sat in front, by the railing, with Umm Ibrahim and the grandmother on two chairs side by side, taking turns holding the baby. Abu Ibrahim's sister sat by herself, looking in a different direction from the rest of them, to a point in the beaten earth track that led to the watchman's hut in the park.

Abu Ibrahim had been a stranger in the building, and so it was with his family. I never saw any of them ringing the bell of the next-door flat. They did not run back and forth between the flats the way most tenants of the building did. They were strangers in the building they had once owned. Abu Ibrahim's father had bought it from a man who took the money and flew to Europe, then sold it to a short, white-haired middle-aged man. He was the new owner, and whenever he wanted to check on it he pressed the al-Kilanis' bell and went in before hearing any greeting.

Abu Ibrahim and the new owner both avoided the neighbours. When they sat together, they talked not only about the building, but about the other neighbourhoods and streets in the city. They would sit facing one another, and speak as if on their guard against anyone else hearing what they were saying.

The building's owner would be silent for a long time, then say something he had just remembered. Abu Ibrahim, also silent, would listen to what he said. They spoke or sat in silence, like a father and his married son waiting for an over-long visit to end.

The building's owner would place two fingers on his chin and pat his jowls, as if no one could rush him into what he was going to say. He would gaze at a point on the wall slightly above Abu Ibrahim's head, and look at the sandy garden of the building in his mind's eye. He looked through the end of the balcony and saw a part of the garden. It was bigger than the space occupied by the building that hid it from the street. There was an empty pool in the middle of it. It was dry and nothing about it hinted at even a memory of water. The watchman's meagre laundry was hung along the top of its cracked circular wall.

In the sandy garden there were also four large palm trees that produced dates in summer. The building's owner had instructed the watchman to distribute half the dates among the tenants. Abu Ibrahim's share was large – he took all the dates from the yellow date tree, and left the fruit from the three other trees for the other tenants.

That was the only prerogative enjoyed by the al-Kilani family. But they felt special, and Abu Ibrahim's mother would rummage through the basin when the watchman, Abu Mahmoud, took the broad basin full of dates from his head and set it on the ground before her. She would stir the dates in the basin around with her cane, dividing them up unequally while pondering the faces of her neighbours in her mind.

With Abu Ibrahim's death, the building's proprietor lost the one home he used to visit. After that, in order for the tenants to pay their rent at the end of every month, they went down to the cotton-clothing store in the Souk Tawila, the market in the old city. They paid the rent to the shopkeeper, who passed it on to the owner.

He was seen, on rare occasions, slowly crossing the street in which the apartment building was located. When he reached the entrance, he would look up at one of the balconies, clasp his hands behind his back, and closely inspect the entrance and the skylights over the stairs.

Abu Ibrahim never had any relationship with his neighbours; not when his father bought it, nor by the time he sold it, nor in the long period when he was content to live in it. It seemed that for him his flat was merely an extension of the al-Munla district located south of the building and from which it was separated by decrepit old buildings and empty lots. In the street to the south at the entrance to al-Munla, and a little before it, were houses whose entrances were filled with potted plants and flowering trees and thresholds of concrete sprinkled with sand. The man from the al-Ghazzawi family stood in front of the house he had built on part of his spacious lot. He was tall, and his round paunch sagged over his torn belt. He stood in the doorway of his grocery shop, all of whose wares were so old as to be no longer edible. He talked to the drivers who passed by, and with his relatives on the balconies of their flats above street level, his back to the door of his shop and the pedestrians on their way to the crowded well-stocked shops further up the street.

Abu Ibrahim's flat was an extension of the street that lay to the south, of its houses with their potted plants, their trees and thresholds so like those houses in the country. Whenever I saw him on the street, just leaving the building, he was always off to chat with someone in their garden, or with another friend sitting on their balcony. Abu Ibrahim al-Kilani had his friends and relatives – you could tell who they were without anyone pointing them out to you. You could recognize them from the gardenia tree in their yard, or the fact that their house was different from those around it, or by the way they sat there quietly on bamboo chairs out on the street, as though the city were still as it once was, a big village on the seashore.

The thick green door was closed on the cold outside. Its coat of dark paint and heavy wood exuded a kind of warmth, which quickly vanished when our gaze fell on the empty sink, on the faucet from which the icy water trickled drop by drop, and on the bare kitchen linoleum whose squares the straw mat was unable to cover.

My older brother was sitting close to me on the mat, and every once in a while he rested his back against the edge of the kitchen cabinet and stretched out his long legs. They looked pale and skinny in the soft, dim light.

They put us in the kitchen, me and him. My little brother was in the living room with our visiting female relatives. Ali and I were in the kitchen. He was quiet and his patience seemed to have run out, when a sound like a dull roar came from the gas stove placed to the side of the sink in front of us.

My aunt came into the kitchen. She did not speak to us, but went straight behind the door to the corner where the linen basket was kept. She put dirty clothes in it and then went to the little pot on the stove. She glanced at it and then retreated to the other room.

My brother Ali was intent on taking care of me, motivated by a precocious sense of responsibility. He was quiet, pursing his lips, making his cheeks seem slack and droopy. Sometimes he didn't know how to express his brotherly feelings, and put his arm around my shoulders as we sat in the kitchen, forcing me to sit up straight on the floor so that I could keep the friendly posture he wanted.

My other aunt, Aliya, came in to prepare something. She stood between the faucet and the rumbling gas stove. She took a few short steps between them and into house slippers in which there were already prints left by her firm feet, which bore down on the delicate new fibres that supported them. This aunt did not say anything to us either, but from time to time she glanced at the small pot on the fire, until steam began to rise and she rushed into the other room for the midwife to tell her what needed to be done.

We did not know which room our mother was in, but something momentous was definitely happening in there. We both knew that whatever it was the scissors and the other metal things in the little pot were going to be used in the process. The handle of the scissors, the part where you put your fingers, was visible over the edge. Ali looked at them and the light in the kitchen dimmed a little; a fleeting melancholy flickered between the two of us, and his lips grew more pursed and his cheeks even droopier than before.

My mother was in one of the two rooms which opened on to one another through a mediating door. She was asleep on her back, in a near coma, while my two aunts moved ever more briskly around the room or left it on some errand on the midwife's orders.

My mother was sleeping, and weak, sweating in her velvety white nightgown. When my aunt came and poured the boiling water out of the little pot, my brother winked at me, and I felt a calm reassurance in the dim kitchen with the thick green door that kept the cold air from leaking in.

My aunt did not allow us to sit in the living room with the female relatives who had gathered for the occasion. One of them came into the kitchen to boil coffee for the ladies, and asked us whether we were hungry, but did not wait for an answer. Then the midwife came in. She did not notice us: she seemed very preoccupied and rushed back to where my mother was, in the room suffused by the heat from the charcoal stove that rose to the ceiling and penetrated the bedclothes.

The closed room was always kept heated. When my aunt Aliya came back into the kitchen her face was red and dripping with sweat. She stood in front of me and opened an upper door of the wooden cupboard. The arch of her foot was slightly fallen, like a little belly. She closed the door and went back out, her feet thudding solidly along the floor.

The midwife frowned as she went about her business in the hot room. As she arrived and went past the doorway of the kitchen, her bulging leather satchel in her hand, my brother Ali had not been able to conceal his fear. She was fat, but walked with great vigour. As soon as she arrived she had started giving orders to my aunt, as if she had appointed a time limit for the birth which was not to be exceeded.

When my mother let out a loud scream, my little brother burst into tears in the living room. His crying erupted all at once, and grew louder and more fierce, and the women were unable to calm him. Ali and I found consolation in his crying. He smiled at me a little, yet remained intensely expectant, as if awaiting our mother's next scream.

It was a girl. My aunts came into the kitchen together, and they were not rejoicing. The midwife called out for them and they hurried back to her. A few moments later, they walked her to the door. She was walking wearily, her bulging leather satchel in her hand. Nabiha al-Shibani, who lived on the fourth floor, came in, bringing a sudden joy into the flat. Nabiha tried to be friendly, and began to talk to our women relatives, whom she did not know very well, some of them not at all.

My father's sister rose to the occasion and talked back to her with equal poise. She enjoyed the situation – she, more than my mother or my aunt Aliya, always spoke in such a way that she could be heard in the al-Shibanis' apartment. She talked with Nabiha as if sharing little secrets with her, or as if resuming a conversation they had begun the day before.

None of the children could imagine what was behind the two windows that overlooked the street. They were shut tight. When one of the shutters was lifted all that could be seen was the white-haired Russian woman's thin face, and, behind her, the darkness of the flat, which made it impossible for anyone peeking in to see anything inside.

The two closed windows were in the same place as the little balconies on the upper floors, but, because the ground floor was so close to the street, just barely above it, the building's architect had decided to create a small garden instead. It was located under the windows. But the white-haired woman with the thin face did not consider the garden a part of her home. She let the soil dry up, and the palm tree in the corner had withered, so on most days of the year it looked like the fossil of a giant tree, a dwarfish stump.

The children from the neighbourhood around the building were plotting something against the Russian family. They shrieked at them, and threw pebbles. The boys grabbed small stones and pieces of wood, or whatever they could lay their hands on, and threw them at the closed wooden shutters. They continued throwing, determinedly, until, at an unexpected moment, the Russian lady opened the shutter of the window, and looked out at the boy caught throwing the stones and the boys around him. She looked at them with no movement in her face or even in her eyes. She stood fixedly and gazed at a point in the midst of them, as if she were thinking of something quite other than the boys or the little rocks that clattered against the window.

The boys stood stock-still where they were, and a thrill of fright ran through their bodies at the sight of the silent, thin face. Even so, they kept looking at it and continued to do so until one of them yelled 'Russian!' followed by another who turned the word into a rhythmic battle cry. Then the children shouted the word a third time, in a chorus, and continued to repeat it while stamping their feet and prancing around the stretch of sidewalk opposite the window, marching back and forth.

It was as if the woman with the thin face was keeping them busy by merely standing at the window. Her daughter came out through the door, and the boys scattered and ran. They raced to the crossroads that led to their own neighbourhoods, and hid behind the walls of the buildings at the crossroads. The tall, stout, blue-eyed Russian girl maintained her walking pace as she chased the boys to the crossroads. She did not once speed up, but took measured steps along the sidewalk. Before she got there, the boys abandoned their posts behind the walls and ran to the next intersection farther up the street, closer to their homes.

The Russian girl approached the complex of streets a short distance before the al-Munla district, and walked with the same purposeful steps. But at some point a few steps before the second intersection, she suddenly stopped. She stood there for a few moments before turning round and going back home in the same way that she had come.

The boys were convinced that the Russian girl trained as a boxer at home. When one of the boys told me that, I could picture a punching bag suspended from the ceiling in one of the rooms in their flat, and her standing in front of it, punching it repeatedly while straining the muscles in her legs, which were planted firmly on the floor.

When the Russian mother left her flat, she followed her usual route, as she had for many years. She was small, and her shoes were like those worn by little girls. She walked quickly, her thin wrinkled face and white hair giving no hint of her urgency. She walked as if she were hurrying to an appointment for which she was late. She walked the same route as her daughter, to the crossroads, and when she got there, she turned into a small side street, avoiding the crowded neighbourhoods. The side street made the distance longer. She arrived at an area of old, half-demolished houses between which there were cultivated allotments of land. She crossed the curving lane, going up the street that led to a sort of hill. On the hill stood an old building; behind it, almost as though they were an extension of it, poor houses stretched down the hill along the crowded street.

The Russian lady went into the building. One of the children saw her as she quickened her steps at the entrance, in her haste to avoid the people whose balconies were stuffed with wood, old wardrobes and rusty pots and tins. The other Russian lady, it was known, was still living in the building, rarely going out, though some of the children had seen her. They said that she looked nothing like the Russian lady in our building, because she was fatter and she smiled at those neighbours she knew. Some of them visited her every so often.

In our building, the Russian lady and her husband never left their flat at the same time. When she went to visit the other Russian lady in her house on the hill her husband stayed at home, alone or with his daughter. He went out before sundown, descending the three steps between his door and the entrance of the building very slowly. He grasped the iron railing in both hands, his back hunched over it. When he reached the bottom of the steps, he stood at the threshold for a few moments. He smoothed his clothes while placing his feet parallel to one another and took his cane, which he had hung on his arm, and grasped its rounded handle in his fist.

When he came out of the house he always headed in the opposite direction his wife had taken. He walked along, staying close to the wall, and when he reached the shop facing the gate of the park, he stopped a little while to rest. When he went on again, anyone watching him knew that he would cross to the opposite sidewalk before reaching the end of the street. He stopped at the same spot every day. He always turned round very slowly, and, slightly dragging his weak leg, crossed the street to the sidewalk and the park fence, walking alongside it.

All I knew of the al-Shibanis' flat was the space that led me from the door to the sitting room. The hallway was empty for the first few steps, and then, curving to the right, it narrowed because of a huge bookcase full of books, pens, photographs, and little pocket notebooks. It was crammed with things that looked to me like gifts.

The door on the left side of the hallway was the way to the kitchen, in which there was no sign of dishes. There was never any food on the table, and no pots or pans on the gas stove which Nabiha al-Shibani had placed directly under the window.

She used to sit on the big couch in the sitting room amid

the tools of her evening amusement: her eyeglasses, women's magazines, and a ball of yarn with two knitting needles. In front of her, a short distance from the couch, stood a low chair she used as a footrest when she stretched out.

If you saw Nabiha sitting or reclining among her evening things, you would think her capable of remaining silent for days, not speaking a word. Even her husband, who was just a few feet away from her, forgot she was in the room, and looked over every so often to check whether she was still there.

He sat facing the wall, his back to the door, through which we used to come into the sitting room. My aunt said that he drank a lot of arak, and swore that more than once she had gone down to their flat on the fourth floor and seen him, his face turned to the wall, and eating in a leisurely way, while seeming to be chatting with someone in the empty chair opposite.

I saw him as well, whenever I entered their flat, sitting on the chair with the little plates of food in front of him. He was friendly. He turned when he saw us coming, and invited us to eat with him, but did not insist, so as not to embarrass my aunt who would not even look at his bottle of arak. I also remember him on the steps, leaning on the black iron railing, or walking slowly between the floors, gasping for breath.

He exchanged greetings with my father. They spoke only a few words but always smiled warmly, until my father led me away and we went up the stairs quickly, leaving him already fumbling for his house key one floor below his own.

At the table he wore special house clothes, to which he devoted much more care than the clothes I saw him wearing

27

on the staircase. He wore a black bathrobe with large embroidered designs. On his feet he had soft slippers that he only
wore while sitting down or walking from room to room.

Nabiha al-Shibani talked to my aunt about the changes
she had decided to make in the sitting room. She stood in the
corner of the room and walked to the table, tracing a line
with her fingers at the height of the cupboard she was going
to order. She gestured at the place where her husband was sitting and said that she would clear it out, except for the
hangings that she would drape from the ceiling to the floor;
and she would put the radio and the record player opposite
that. Said al-Shibani looked at the wall in front of him, and
every now and then asked my aunt brief, concise questions
about the building, or else about the water, the neighbours,
her husband's line of business.

When Nabiha al-Shibani spoke at length, it was an unac-
customed thing for her, for she normally stayed silent amidst
her evening clutter. When she talked, she talked without pausing, her neck puffed up, her shoulders slightly hunched
forward, making her look slender and excitable.

She moved gracefully despite the fact that she was past
fifty. When she went to the kitchen to prepare coffee for my
aunt, she took swift, widely spaced steps so that her long legs
seemed out of keeping with the upper half of her body.

The sitting room became cosy and bright when Nabiha al-
Shibani talked a lot, so much so that I wasn't in the least
embarrassed to sit at one end of the big sofa while she sat at
the other. This room was the only place in the apartment for
visitors because Nabiha was always talking about rearranging
and replacing the furniture. Each time she did so, I too would
find myself imagining moving back the big sofa, the chairs,

and the wide table, and putting them in the corner in front of the staircase, ready for the porters to come and put them on a truck to take them away.

Only the sitting room was familiar to me. The hallway and the bookcase in the dim light, bristling with books, photographs, little palm-sized notebooks, always remained as unfamiliar as the first time I had seen it.

When Katya stopped to pick up a book, she spent a long time flipping through pages, notebooks, book covers. She came from the bedrooms, coming the long way through the living room and the entrance hall. She ran her fingers along the wood of the shelves. When she peered up on to the top shelf, she hesitated a little, then strained her body upward, her dress rising above her plump thighs.

Katya greeted my aunt as if she were about to fall asleep or had just woken up, and went back to her room through the hallway and living room. She crossed the cold living room, which was normally kept locked, paying no attention to the furniture set around its walls and in its corners. Her feet would cross the warm carpet, and when she reached her room she paid no attention to her sister reclining on her bed or to her brother reading at his desk in the next room.

My mother tried so many times to change the rooms around. She said that she could not relax in the flat. There was a room at the front and a room at the back, and it was as if she were in two flats separated from one another. My aunt ignored my mother's repeated attempts, because her own two rooms were set back far from the sound of her children's chaos and running about. She locked them up and put her children out in the small hallway that ran between them and that led to the bathroom. But when she was in the kitchen or on the big balcony, her children opened the hall door leading on to the parlour. They went in there and spread themselves around in it, especially in the narrow spaces behind the sofas.

My mother tidied the flat a hundred times a day. She complained that everyone coming in from outside only came into our open rooms. My cousins, too, raised havoc in the room next door to our parlour when my mother was in the other room, the one beside the kitchen.

My aunt kept her two rooms locked. Even her sofas in the living room were less likely to be used than ours. My bachelor uncle, my father's business partner, was content merely to ask her for small services, while my mother – who was so busy and absorbed in her chores that she hardly had time to talk – looked after his bed, his laundry, and the rest of his things.

My aunt and mother were always thinking of changing the situation of both families in the flat. My mother was waiting for my father's brother to get married and move out; my aunt was also waiting for him to move, and for us to move with him.

Once she had said to my mother, after an argument, that she had been in this building before us. But the flat had become two flats, for ever: the kitchen had two cupboards, two refrigerators, and two gas stoves; there were two sets of furniture in the parlour, and separate bedrooms. As to the two bathrooms, one Arab and one in the Western style, they agreed on a schedule that regulated the laundry and other uses of it, and the children took turns bathing.

My mother longed for the days of Wasila and Umm Habib. She said that back then we were one family, and the flat was one flat, so much so that no one knew in which room they would end up sleeping. Abu Habib recognized where he was going to sleep only by where his mattress was placed. One time he came in very tired, undressed, and climbed under

31

the covers, beside my aunt – she did not even realize what was happening until she put her hand on his chest. My mother described how Abu Habib flew out of bed, panic-stricken, and how he refused, that night, to sleep anywhere but on the balcony.

In those days – my mother said – it was as if we were still back in the village. Abu Habib was always joking, and his wife was good-hearted and she joked along with him. Now, on the other hand, no one could stand one another. She said that my aunt now wished to live like the Christian, Armenian and foreign tenants in the building, and was ashamed if any of them came to visit us in our flat.

In the old building, which was in the area near the river, the landlord used to gather the tenants every night on the roof, which he had furnished with flowerpots, mats, and cushions, and which was lit with bulbs strung from a line that ran from the wooden entrance to its high edge. The landlord, Abu Musa al-Khatib, wore a long white robe, and was never without his hookah, the mouthpiece ornamented with small pearls. He was generous, and talked about legendary exploits and acts of heroism the most recent of which had occurred many centuries ago.

Coffee was served to us as we sat or lay on the floor. This was how the tenants spent their evening, for their day started early. All my relatives occupied the two apartments on the first floor. There were so many of them that if you had wanted to count them, you would have kept making mistakes. The rooms were spacious, because there was no furniture in them, but there was unceasing movement among the rooms, the two kitchens and two bathrooms, and the entrance to the floor, which separated the two apartments. They were as happy and cheerful as if they were on vacation, or were living in some temporary quarters, after which each would be going back home. They were so cheerful that none of them ever thought of going off and being alone, even when that was possible. They had left the village and behaved as if they were on an outing to Beirut.

The building stood on a street that ran along the length of the river and was crowded with working men who wore thick long garments and black or khaki kaffiyehs on their heads. They crossed the street or crowded the middle of it, gathering into groups dispersed every so often by processions of cattle or sheep going to the slaughterhouse just beyond the curve of the street, near the building. The smell of grilled meat rose from the restaurant across the way. The men crowded into it, spilling out on to the street, forced to sit at tables on the sidewalk.

There was also a bakery in the building opposite, brightly lit and noisy all night long. Its customers came from the overcrowded tin houses on the edge of the river.

A herd of cattle crossed the muddy road, leaving droppings and urine the length and breadth of the street; the stench rose up to the roofs. The entrance to our building was very large, as if it were a plaza in an open space instead of a walled-in enclosure. People coming in were faced with a long walkway. And the open space of the entrance was piled with canvas bags filled with straw, bought by Abu Musa al-Khatib to resell to the cattle traders in the slaughterhouse.

The building was no longer habitable. On the wide flat roof there was a separate room built like a small stone hut. The wood of its door and window frames and shutters was now cracked and rotten. From that height, the big park looked much farther away. The roof was more than one storey above our flat. Rusty spots showed all over the cement floor and walls of the room and the low cement wall running around the roof, in round, regular blotches. Neither the tenants on the lower floors, nor Mathilde nor her third-floor neighbour, had been up to the roof for a long time. Every time she passed it, Madame Laure would shy away from the large iron door that opened on to the roof from the fifth floor. The iron door

34

was locked, and the people in the building paid no attention to the antennae whose shafts had fallen down, or the television aerials, once held aloft by the shafts, which had fallen apart.

Only Madame Gadijian knew that she had to pack her bags, gather up her belongings, and leave. No one knew why she had decided to do it. They did not believe that her husband had just grown too tired of walking up five flights: he was thin and small and always moved briskly, hurrying energetically from room to room. Nor had Madame Gadijian had any problems with the landlord or any of the tenants. No one knew why she left the building with her husband and two daughters – they did not even linger to say goodbye to their neighbours.

When it was empty, their home looked like an entirely different place. The wallpaper in the two bedrooms had been ruined by the water that leaked on to the walls from the water tank in the roof space. The two doors that led to the two little balconies were broken at the bottom. And in the kitchen, the plastic paper with which Madame Gadijian had covered the small cabinets and marble shelving was faded and old. She had decided long ago to leave the building, even before Madame Laure had gone ahead with the repairs in her own flat, which included tiling the floor of her cement balcony.

Madame Gadijian took all the tenants by surprise. It was as if her family were the only one that had ever left its home and moved into another. After the big lorry drove away, carrying the last load of furniture, the neighbours began to inspect the steps and the iron rails of the balcony and some other points visible from the building entrance. The departure of the Gadijian family made them realize that their building was

no longer new. Madame Laure, in her subsequent conversations about houses, would always now mention how old
they were. Nabiha al-Shibani talked about the good qualities
of old buildings: how the light filled the rooms, how spacious
the rooms were and how high the ceilings, but she could not
help adding that the building next door was clean because it
had been built more recently.

The al-Kilani family paid no attention to those parts that
showed the building's age. Perhaps they knew that they were
no longer in a new building, though they changed none of
their habits. The upholsterer still came to their flat every so
often, as he always had. The potted plants stayed, the kind
that grew like creepers, spreading along every corner of the
rear balcony.

Sulayman the milkman went with his family up to the
Gadijian flat. He walked up the steps at the front, followed by
his two sons, who were as plump as he was, with their mother
coming up behind. Sulayman greeted whomever he met on
the stairs, and so did his sons and his panting wife. Mathilde
did not move when the woman approached her, her posture
showing clearly what she thought the neighbourhood was
coming to. Mathilde gripped the metal doorknob as if she
wanted to go back inside her flat, but something held her
back.

The woman followed her husband and two sons, walking
ahead of her on the stairs. Sulayman went through the door
of the empty flat, and was followed by the sons who so resembled him. The woman entered. The elder son, dressed in a
grey suit and blue necktie, greeted my aunt from the rear balcony. He was well-mannered, but my aunt missed Madame
Gadijian's husband, who would never have come out on to

the balcony and surprised her like that. He knew the rudiments of good behaviour: when he came out on the balcony, he would knock, and look down at something in the vicinity of his feet, never changing that posture until my aunt took the initiative and greeted him. Only then would he raise his head, smiling and timid.

Nabiha al-Shibani said that Sulayman knew that Madame Gadijian would leave the flat, which was why in recent days he had been watching the windows and balconies more intently than ever. It was as if he were waiting for just the right moment to go to the landlord. Perhaps he had reached an agreement with him already, before Madame Gadijian had made her final decision.

Sulayman succeeded in convincing the landlord to accept the small rent which was all he could pay. He reminded him about the building's ruined staircase, and told him that these days proprietors were putting in elevators even before the apartments were built.

The next day, Sulayman got out of the car he never tired of polishing. He stood at his car door, which he left ajar, and looked back down the street. The lorry with the furniture looked as though it were carrying far more than was safe. The porters began to unload all the goods. Madame Laure remarked, while listening to the noise of the movers and the clinking of all the bottles, that Sulayman should reserve a room for the milk containers, and Nabiha al-Shibani told my aunt that she was still waiting to hear the mooing of a cow that would surely be part of the furniture.

My aunt, who was taking part in the endless debate among the tenants on Sulayman and his family, told them how he only buttoned his trousers once he was out on the balcony, and how he strained with his short arm to buckle his belt.

My mother could never be sure that my aunt was not discussing our household business in front of the neighbours. Sometimes she used to tell my father to talk in a very low voice so that my aunt would not be able to hear and then tell the neighbours what was going on.

The people in the building had been most eager to talk when our relatives had first arrived. My grandfather preceded us with our other relatives. He led the long procession up the stairs. He was wearing his collarless shirt, and behind him the line of men, women, and children extended all the way down the flights of stairs to the next floor. Not knowing whether he should greet the women who came to look at him from behind the glass doors, he proceeded to the fifth floor without pausing on the staircase, never speaking or looking behind him. He came up as if he and the procession behind him were simply crossing the street from one house to another, or as if they were going to turn around as soon as they arrived at the top and head straight back down the stairs.

According to my grandfather, he had to frown and keep silent in order to resist the face of the blonde French woman who gazed at him from behind her door. He saw her out of the corner of his eye, with his back stooped a little, his wide palms dangling just a little above his knees. Abu Habib and my aunt's husband and the rest of the procession looked as if they were in the middle of some long journey. They had all given in to my grandfather, who was the elder of the family, and who was compensating, with his frowning and his silence, for their tendency to frivolity and readiness to make chitchat on the stairs.

My grandfather entered the door of the flat at the top of the house, followed by the others, while the tenants drew away from the doors and went back into their rooms. My grandfather went into the spacious, empty hall of the flat. The men and women separated into groups around the rooms, and the children ran to the balconies. My grandfather called for my aunt and she appeared. He pointed to the middle of the salon and told her, 'I want to sleep here.'

From the poor district near the river straight to this building: that was a social distance only my grandfather would hazard, with his passion for spacious rooms, and his daring to make light of the differences between districts and people. My grandfather, who rested his head against the wall in deep thought before falling asleep, would never know the chaos that he had stirred up in the building. The women went around knocking on each other's doors and talking rapidly, as if what they had seen on the stairs was a ghastly mistake that could still be corrected. He had pondered sadly, his head bowed, the fact that my father was in one flat and he in another.

The French family living on the fourth floor was less disapproving than the other tenants. The French woman smiled at my aunt, who was hanging her laundry on the kitchen balcony. My aunt responded with a smile and rushed back to Umm Habib and the others. There was so much noise and talking going on that the French woman smiled a second time at Umm Habib, who had gone out to look for herself.

From that day onwards, all the men, women, and children in the flat flashed broad smiles whenever they saw a member of the French family. In the summer, the French sent ice cubes to my aunt for her to put in the water pitcher, while they in turn were delighted by the flat loaves of bread and country eggs from our village that my grandfather sent.

But they didn't stay long. They had come for a fixed period and they knew it. Their furniture was temporary, and they never put even a single potted plant on their kitchen balcony. When they left the building they took away only their clothes; they left the refrigerator and other household things behind, as they had agreed with the landlord. The French woman took her books with her, but left the glossy magazines with the colourful covers. They lay in a heap in front of the door after she had gone.

Once my uncle had joined the boxing club, the only time we ever saw him was when he was going up or down the stairs. He would race down, waving one hand high as he swerved around the landings between floors; in his other hand he held his sturdy black leather gym bag.

From the time he joined the boxing club, that was all he cared about. He came home from the bakery and took off his flour-whitened clothes, washed his face and ears, combed his hair with water, went to the closet to get his dark blue jacket with the metal buttons, and did up the middle button. He looked at himself in the big closet mirror and considered his reflection, as if a photographer had asked him to hold still.

Then he suddenly pulled his hands apart, as if about to draw two pistols hanging at his sides, drew them up level with his face and began to shadow-box in front of the mirror.

He calmed down a little, smoothed his hands over his jacket, then suddenly began to punch again, fiercely, as if someone had provoked him or punched him unexpectedly.

He used to ask my brother to put up his hands. My brother would stand there rather warily, hesitating, while my uncle rained jabs and punches on his hands. My uncle never stayed still. Sweat poured off him whenever he looked into a room packed with people talking.

My father warned him about overdoing his boxing training outside the club, especially in areas where there were lots of strangers. He did listen to my father, but was quick to forget. He carried his sturdy gym bag, raced down the stairs, stopped at a certain point on the steps, dropped his bag to the floor, and began to shadow-box.

He had been standing in front of the door to the bakery when Adairaki was passing by. Adairaki had looked admiringly at my uncle's height and suggested that he come along to the club. At first, he had not liked the training; he got very tired, as the time he spent there was at the cost of his sleep. Initially he had hesitated to go – until it became a habit. He then bought his blue jacket, whose upper-half bore, on the breast pocket, the multicoloured embroidered emblem of the club.

His height would be of great advantage to him, Adairaki had explained. None of the other boxers of his weight could block his blows to their faces; that was the truth. In the photographs he brought from the club, his opponent was shorter, staring intently at my uncle's stomach, which was at the level of his face or just a little lower. My uncle held his head high, and his eyes open in a way that never would have suggested he was boxing. He was looking aside at the photographer, which made his long nose stand out prominently from his narrow face.

Adairaki said that my uncle, because he was so tall, had to be careful of his stomach; he had to protect his abdomen. My father imagined what the pain of a strong punch to the stomach would feel like; he rubbed the spot on his own stomach where he felt his chronic ulcer pains.

Once he was very late. My aunt waited up for him; it was late night when she heard the sound of a car parking at the entrance of the building. She ran to the door and looked out on to the landing. My uncle was still wearing his glossy boxing trunks and high-top training shoes. A blood-stained towel lay around his shoulders. He looked feeble and exhausted on the stairs, held up between Adairaki and another boxer from the club. 'They really hurt him this time,' Adairaki said as my uncle put his head under the faucet and the water flowed into the sink, pink with blood.

When my father asked him what the point of boxing was, he had no answer. He kept quiet and nodded or shook his head in response to my father's stream of questions. However, after he began to take part in matches at the club, and got the serious wound to his head, he no longer trained in front of the mirror, or anywhere at all in the flat. He walked placidly down the stairs without his leather bag, which he now left at the club, never bringing it home except when he wanted to wash his sweat-stained kit.

When my uncle beat the Iranian champion, my father was sitting in the front row. There were layers of electric light bulbs suspended from the high ceiling, and the smell of the long hall was suffused with sweat as the spectators exchanged boxing talk, some of which my father had heard from my uncle. The bell rang, and the two boxers approached the middle of the ring. My father's tension turned into pains in his own stomach. The Iranian champion was brown-skinned and had a large head, and aimed his punches at my uncle's chest and stomach. My uncle began to retreat back towards the ropes, in a series of light hops, keeping his head and hands moving. He moved in and out without laying a glove on his opponent, as if he was putting on a show. The Iranian abandoned the earnest manner with which he had begun the match, and began to stroll and feint almost casually, as if his mind were on something far beyond the ring.

No one understood how my uncle beat the Iranian champion. He put his athletic robe over his glossy, short trunks, picked up his towel, and came to the flat accompanied by my aunt's husband and my father, who was bragging about his victory. He looked like a giant when he appeared in the doorway. He rested a little on the chair, then he went to the sink, which cracked in the middle when he threw his leg over it.

When he returned victorious from Greece, my grandfather insisted on having a celebration in his honour in our village back in the South. All the villagers came together in the courtyard of the house and on the balconies nearby, and on the roofs. The teenagers set off firecrackers, and the local band made a circle around the table in the courtyard. His silver trophy stood on the table, with a giant cucumber next to it on the white tablecloth. My uncle said that it was one of the smallest cucumbers in Greece.

The villagers stared at the cucumber, engrossed in talk of cucumber seeds and modern agriculture, of how all the fruit and vegetables in Greece were so huge. And one of the villagers said that he had once seen a banana twice as long as the cucumber.

When my relatives had processed up the stairs, among all the women only Mathilde had not been driven by curiosity to stare at the new arrivals. She had heard the tread and shuffling of many feet, and peeked out from behind the lead of the glass door, then closed it and went off to finish a chore she had already begun.

When the women began to knock on one another's doors, a few minutes after my grandfather entered the door of our flat, Mathilde was not among them. No one saw Mathilde except in the early evening, walking the short distance to the door of the second apartment on the same floor.

Mathilde was in the habit of visiting Madame Khayyat.

She went from her door to her neighbour's door, taking four steps going and four coming back. The only person she liked was Madame Khayyat, who was also tall and quiet, and who, also like her, rationed her greetings to her immediate neighbours in the building.

Mathilde and Madame Khayyat appeared to be least flexible towards newcomers, and, as a result of their neighbours' more tolerant attitude, began to close their doors and stop all visiting. Madame Khayyat was rarely seen any more, and no one had a clear idea of when she was staying up in the mountain and when she was staying in the building.

They only ever saw Mathilde in the small space of hallway that separated her flat from her immediate neighbour's. She responded to anyone who greeted her, but smiled at no one. From the very first time my aunt – my father's sister – had talked to her, her facial features had indicated that she was not prepared to get involved in social niceties. On that first occasion, my aunt had proceeded on her way upstairs directly to the flat, without ringing Nabiha al-Shibani's doorbell as she usually did when coming home from her little trips to the world outside.

Mathilde paid no attention to the children going up the stairs; it was as if she did not see or hear them. She put her key in the lock and turned it while wiping her feet before opening the door. She was fifty years old, with piercing blue eyes that seemed even harsher because of the puffiness of the delicate skin around them. She hardly spoke. When the children heard her say something to her neighbour, they noticed that her voice lacked the gentleness of a woman's voice – it was like the voice of a man who had just got out of bed. And Mathilde was more like the men in the building. She was like them in the way she greeted people and even, a little, in her appearance. In the past, the women in the building had used to say that she sat at a table in the evening and gambled at cards with strange men. The women also said that she never went to bed until the early hours of the morning, and that the man who stood in front of his little car in front of the building had known her before her husband had died.

He looked childish in his velvet trousers and plimsolls as he stood by the door of his Gordini car. He reached inside the open window and honked the horn lightly while looking up at the balcony on Mathilde's floor.

My mother was revolted by his soft, ruddy face, which looked as though it had just been fried, and by Mathilde, who consented to go out on the balcony to see him.

My mother saw Mathilde only rarely; the first time she saw her she had considered it her duty to greet her. She had spoken a few words and continued on her way up the stairs without being sure whether or not she had heard a response.

She just did not understand Mathilde, or the tall, quiet Madame Khayyat, who acted as though she lived in a different building. She did not know how to talk to them, and began to criticize my aunt, who always made such an effort to look nice in front of them. She said that my aunt was copying Nabiha al-Shibani when she talked, and that she had started to affect a comical nasal twang whenever she was speaking to Madame Laure from her balcony.

The quarrels between my mother and my aunt grew louder. It seemed as if each had memorized her part and waited for the precise cue to begin to play it. At first they shouted at the same time, and one could not hear what the other was saying, but when the first outburst had died down, my mother began to complain and curse the children and her bad luck. She began to wish she were dead; while my aunt shouted back her own harsh words, my mother's face streamed with hot tears.

My mother did not like the building. She was only happy when she gazed out at the tops of the china bark trees from the open balcony doors. She sat alone, yet somehow as if she were with other women, as if listening to other women seated around her and speaking very quietly. She had been alone in the building ever since Wasila and Umm Habib went away. There was only her and the children, and my father came home late at night, utterly exhausted, and fell asleep even before she had reheated his supper. He dozed off, leaning his head and shoulders against the wall, his high boots placed side by side on the floor near him.

In the building down by the river, the rooms had never been quiet: Wasila would fight with Mustafa Jawad and throw him on to the floor; my Aunt Aliya began dolling herself up at noon in anticipation of an evening visit from her Beiruti cousin. Yusuf prepared the platters of nut pastry in the flat before sending them to the bakery, where they were baked for him to sell outside his door. My grandfather visited infrequently, and when he did enter the room my aunt shooed away the children, Zardakhan and Muhammad Said. During the nightly gatherings on the flat roof Abu Musa al-Khatib seemed taller than the other men up there, and the smell of straw wafted up from the entrance, making the place seem even warmer.

My mother, Zardakhan, and my Aunt Aliya went down the big staircase. When they reached the outer entrance they stood behind the door to check for the last time that their clothes were decent. Aunt Aliya set her foot over the wooden threshold of the door and started down the street. The other women followed her out and walked sedately in the direction of the huge old brick slaughterhouse that seemed to them like a single enormous room.

They were careful to avoid stepping into the shiny, squishy mud of the street, and did their best to stay to the side, for when the cows passed by and one of them raised her tail to drop manure or spout urine, their discomfort in the street grew even worse. They pushed up their headcoverings a little, and trained their eyes straight ahead to a point on the great brick structure, which still seemed far away despite the distance they had come.

They kept to the side of the street because the middle of the street was occupied by wagons passing by or groups of men in kaffiyehs and khaki clothes. They were the first to arrive in the area from the country, and the families that lived in the houses on either side of the street seemed as though they were still engrossed in unpacking.

They turned left before reaching the brick building, into a quiet street into which apartment blocks, tin-roofed houses, and the throngs of customers coming from the slaughterhouse had never intruded. They proceeded down the street, which grew quieter the farther they went. They could even hear the wind blowing at one point, and beside the asphalt Zardakhan saw a patch of green grass and little yellow flowers. Now they spread out, no longer concerned about one another, as if the street stretched before them, as if they were on their way to different destinations.

Before coming to the French hospital they turned off to the

right and walked on the unpaved earth. Zardakhan could no longer walk steadily on the smooth oval white pebbles. My aunt scented the smell of the sea and gazed leisurely at its calm surface, as smooth as oil. My mother was content to stroll down close to the strip that divided the water from the fine gravel. It was enough for her to smell the mass of sluggish water and urge her two companions to come closer to it. They came closer, stumbling in their effort not to fall down on to the beach, littered with rags and the remnants of tyres and rusty tins. They turned back towards the asphalted road and stood again on the pavement, not knowing what to do to fill the time for the rest of their outing.

No one could guess what sort of things Mathilde and Madame Khayyat talked about. They sat, one on the bed and the other on the narrow boudoir chair. Mathilde leaned over. The puffy skin around her eyes sagged a little as she caught a glimpse of herself in the mirror.

She listened, and spoke a little, and after a time stood up as if surprised at the length of time they had spent together. She offered a brief word of parting and went back to her flat.

When Madame Khayyat visited her, Mathilde occupied herself by imagining the small changes she might make in the placement of her furniture and of the pictures on the wall. They sat apart, one at each end of the great sofa.

Mathilde rose to brew some coffee. She held the end of the long-handled coffee pot in her hand, keeping the fire underneath it low and flickering. Madame Khayyat's cup sat on top of the little end-table beside the sofa. Despite their frequent visits to one another, they usually began by inquiring about distant relatives.

Mathilde closed the doors and the wooden shutters. She also locked the glass-leafed doors between the rooms and turned on an electric lamp. She and Madame Khayyat sat in the soft light that made them feel as though it were already evening. Madame Khayyat left the wooden door to her bedroom open, and when Mathilde had occasion to sit on the narrow stool at the dressing table she could hear the sounds of passing cars and the cries of people strolling in the park.

Mathilde, when she sat on her bed amid her coats and hats, never allowed herself to feel that she was all alone in the flat, so she did not curl her feet up beneath her on the bed. She sat with them straight out before her, and that severe look never left her face.

But when she was in her bed she forgot the building and its tenants and even the people who came to stroll in the park from the crowded street nearby.

The furniture in the room was as it had always been. The bedside table was still in the corner to the right of the bed, and her pink robe hung from a hook on one side of the wardrobe door, an old overcoat she had left there ages ago hung on the other side.

Mathilde, in her locked room among her unchanging furniture, thought she should get out of bed elegantly; she placed her toes on the floor, and stepped lightly across to the hanging robe, which she wore when out on the balcony.

The room was still as it always had been: Mathilde had done nothing but dust the chest of drawers, bedside table, and bedstead. Nothing had changed in the room. Even the edge of the magazine sticking out over the top of the chest of drawers was still in the spot where it had been put long ago.

In spite of that, though, she was seized with anxiety when her gaze fell upon a patch of land to the rear of the building. The roof of the watchman's house was piled with old boards, trash, and threadbare clothes. The watchman no longer looked after the flowers in front of the door, and the green plants dried up because he watered them so infrequently.

The same anxiety touched her when she looked at the large house next door, separated from her building only by a stone wall. There, the woman who lived on the top floor kept only a single window open, keeping all the other windows and doors shut tight. Then Mathilde felt lonely in the room, and the brass bed frame that stood near the window seemed to concentrate an intense cold in itself.

Madame Khayyat was Mathilde's only friend. The other tenants knew that she did nothing but open and close her door, and that when she wanted to go to her neighbour's flat, she would always ask herself whether it was a good time to do so. She never went up to the fourth floor, where Madame Laure and Nabiha al-Shibani were engrossed in imagining new ways of moving the furniture around their rooms. There was constant animation and movement in the two fourth-floor apartments, where the two women passed the time gossiping about the balconies opposite. Madame Khayyat opened and closed her flat, kept quiet or spoke a little, depending upon the look on Mathilde's face.

And in the tiny space between her door and her neighbour's,

Madame Khayyat stood, waiting for Mathilde to open the door, grasping the metal doorknob, and glancing at the stairwell if she heard a footstep on the stairs. Mathilde, for her part, crossed the short distance imperturbably. She stood in front of the other apartment and peered through the crack in the door that she knew would open momentarily, and through which Madame Khayyat would peer, wrapped in her long black robe.

Mathilde had moments which she never shared with her neighbour. Madame Khayyat knew this from the way Mathilde rose from her dressing table and hurried to the door. She would lie alone on her bed, gazing out at the park and the strollers in it. She would get up and go out into the kitchen or on to the back balcony, and after a while she would begin to think that the time had come to go up to her daughter's house, up in the mountain.

Mathilde kept to herself. Her neighbour thought that she was waiting for the man with the Gordini, honking its horn after he had parked it alongside the kerb. She kept to herself even after his visits became less and less frequent. On the last few occasions he had honked the horn just once. He would wait in the car until she looked out over the balcony. When he saw her, he would raise his hand in greeting and nod slightly, then restart the engine of the car and move slowly away.

My grandfather didn't stay long in the flat. Not only that, but his preparations for his return to the village took no more than a few minutes. My aunt simply packed him a bundle of his clothes, he took it up and walked down the stairs. And when she saw, from the balcony, that he had covered a good distance in the direction of the market and the car that was waiting to take him away, she rushed to the corner where he had been sleeping, took his rolled-up mattress to another room, and pulled out of the wall the nails on which he used to hang his clothes.

Ever since he arrived from the village he had known that he would not stay long in Beirut. Even when saying goodbye to my grandmother in the village, he had given her all kinds of detailed instructions, as if he would be back a few days later.

What had kept him so long was setting up the bakery. In the salon where he slept he would get up before dawn. He would jump up off his mattress, as if he had been restless and awake for a long time, anxious about the day, put on his clothes, and stand at the door of the room where my aunt was sleeping with her husband. He would wake her by calling her a few times, then, when she woke up, tell her that he was leaving and would not be back until that evening.

Once he started working in the bakery, he made it back home late every night. He worked much harder than my father or uncle. He did as much work as both of them combined. He would fill the big kneading trough with flour and water, and start in. His big fists worked what would slowly become a stiff dough, which he would place on the shelf for the worker who would divide it into smaller lumps.

He spent most of his day at this trough, looking every so often through the little window at my father waiting on the customers. He would often go to check on the oven and chat with the cook who hung back from the opening and the flames licking out.

At night, my aunt set out his food on a big plate. She would serve him huge portions and always created a quiet place for him so that he would not be distracted from eating. He drank a great deal of water from the pitcher at his side, his back braced against the wall.

Wasila and Umm Habib swore that, the whole time he lived in the flat, he never once went out on to the balcony overlooking the park. But in the blazing hot summer days before he returned to the village, he had gone out on to the big kitchen balcony, and sat in the cool breeze there. He had sat for a long time on the chair near the potted plants; my grandmother had sent the seeds of those plants from the village.

That was the only time he sat out on the balcony. He did not see a single one of the neighbours in the tier of balconies running down the building. When my aunt told him how the French woman had smiled at her, he smiled gently and said he wished that he could see one of the French neighbours for himself.

The French woman smiled for him too. After that, he said that the French were better than all the Arabs in the building, and told my aunt to give them some of what my grandmother sent us from the village. He maintained that they loved our food.

He was dripping with sweat when two women came into the bakery. They asked my father for bread, and while he was busy preparing it they stood gazing at what was happening behind the little window. My grandfather was pounding the dough with both hands, the sweat glistening on his bare chest. He lifted the huge batch of dough in his hands, and manipulated it as if it weighed nothing. They continued to look at him and whisper softly until my father came back to the counter.

My grandfather said that the woman's evil eye had struck him. He had just finished putting the water on the flour to prepare the second batch of dough when he felt pain spread through his right arm. The pain was so strong that it almost threw him to the ground. He went home, still in pain, and though my aunt massaged hot oil into his arm, shoulder, and part of his back, it did no good.

In the morning, my father took him to the French hospital near our old flat in the river quarter. The doctor who treated him was a Frenchman wearing delicate eyeglasses. He was very friendly and began to laugh when the interpreter told him that my grandfather had been afflicted by the evil eye of a woman who looked at him through the hatch between the room where he mixed the dough and the counter where my father stood. As he was lifting the dough and as she was talking to her friend, he realized that she . . . And the interpreter called on God's protection.

The lancing pain in his arm grew worse. The people from our village took him to a big hospital nearer our flat. Grandfather had never even known it was there. He went along, and there the doctor decided to operate on his arm at the elbow joint.

Grandfather could not bear to stay very long among the nurses and the rooms that smelled sourly of medicine. He begged the doctor to release him, and when he saw there was nothing doing, he began to work on the nurses.

He eventually told my father to take him home immediately. It was hot in the sitting room where he slept. He went out on to the large balcony, and while he stood looking at the plants in their earthenware pots, he decided to go back to the village and never to return to Beirut.

My aunt's husband loved being a cab driver, and he loved his taxi, which he always parked carefully in the shade of the great wall of the park. Before going into the building, he took what he thought to be a last look at the shiny grille of the car and its gleaming doors, but as he mounted the steps he looked back again, and again from the window at each landing of the staircase, until he finally reached the flat. He had hair that was combed to a quiff, two-tone shoes that were always clean and shiny, and a moustache trimmed narrow and straight.

My aunt began to get suspicious of the affected tone that had crept into his voice and his visits to photographers who posed him like a film star. In the pictures, his eyes were limpid and dewy, and his facial complexion perfect, all wreathed in a kind of imperceptible glow.

Everyone in the flat noticed how his accent had begun to change. My father said that he talked like the young spivs who lounged around outside the movie-house on Mousaitbeh Street, with whom he spent more and more time. Nabiha al-Shibani never hid her admiration – she said he was the most beautiful man in the building, and every so often she warned my aunt of the dangerous consequences of his night work. Who took taxis home at that hour, she said, except for women coming home from bars?

He was scrupulous about keeping his handkerchief pressed and folded, and now bought all kinds of soap, shaving cream and colognes. He stored them in his dresser drawer, transfer-ring the little tubs and tubes, one at a time, to the ledge of the mirror above the sink in the bathroom.

When he was with my real uncle, he would stand on the little balcony overlooking the park, his foot on the iron of the decorative railings, and begin to talk, gesturing with his hand as if teaching a class. He would make a round 'o' with two fin-gers and lower his hand sententiously, as if that way he could moderate my uncle's weakness and recklessness. My uncle would listen, standing tall and straight, but when anyone passed through the next room or stuck their head out on the balcony opposite, they fell silent and looked down together at the street.

Sometimes they left the balcony and went down the stairs, still talking. They would get into the gleaming taxi and set off as if they were going on some important mission, and then come back as if they had suddenly decided to abort it.

My aunt, preoccupied with her visits to the al-Shibani family and Madame Laure, paid little attention to him. She said that he had always loved nice clothes from the time he was a boy. Even so, she could be sharp with him when she saw him standing entranced in front of the mirror, adjusting his shirt collar from behind to cover his neck more elegantly.

When his late nights grew more and more frequent, all she could do was wait for him. She would sit on her bed in the dark for hours, without moving. When he came in, she would ask him what time it was, then pull the covers over her head, and curl up in the bed. She was content with that small protest, but it made no impression on him. He would take off his trousers and shirt and go to sleep in the other room.

As soon as he left the room, she would get out of bed and begin to search his pockets, looking for some evidence to confirm the suspicions that now seemed inescapable, counting the money in his pocket, smelling the notes, and examining the sleeves of his shirt.

Nabiha al-Shibani had advised her to dress up for him and fuss over him when he was at home. She acted on this advice and began, in the early afternoon, to send the children to the park, and to lock as many doors as she could. He would be drinking his coffee and staring out at the tall trees in the park, lost in thought. He did not look at her. Perhaps he could not soften at seeing that she'd had Nabiha al-Shibani freshen her make-up for her, or perhaps he was afraid he would give something away if he were to look at her or speak to her.

My aunt was not really convinced by Nabiha al-Shibani's advice; she could detect not the slightest change in him, but every time her patience was exhausted and she was ready to explode, she would check herself at the last minute.

But when she saw with her own eyes the print of red lips on his handkerchief, she could not wait for morning to come. She raged at him, but he pretended to be asleep and murmured plaintively and indistinctly. She raised her voice again and shook his head on the pillow. That woke him, and within seconds, their shouts and cries had woken up everyone in the house. My father was at that time sleeping at the bakery. My mother stood behind the door, not daring to enter the room, while my uncle stood between them, with one hand over his sister's mouth, and with the other, fending off her husband, who kept trying to get at her, and then backing off.

In the morning, she wanted to go up to the village to tell my grandfather, and also asked my father and uncle, as her brothers, to put an end to her husband's misbehaviour. Finally she decided to bar him from the flat or seeing his children. He did not find this too oppressive. He took away a few of his things, which he threw together hurriedly, and rushed down the stairs without so much as a glance at his children, huddled around their mother.

He did not come back that afternoon, or that night, nor the next day nor any of the days after that. Twice or three times he parked his taxi behind the intersection in front of the park. My uncle went over to him, and they spent some time sitting together talking in the car. Before they parted, he started up his engine and drove twice round the park. My uncle got out a short distance from the building and went up to the flat, heading straight out on to the small balcony and evading all curious looks and inquiries.

In his absence, my aunt took exquisite care of the children. She went down to Nabiha al-Shibani's flat only rarely. She never asked about her husband, or so it seemed, and once when he came back to take some more of his things, she ignored his presence and went on making up the bed in the other room, not far from where he was.

My father was the one who brought him back after he had been gone for some time. He had grown thinner, his head seemed too big for his body; it was as if he had come back from the country to the city. He put down on the sofa the bag he had bought while he was away, and sat alone in the living room. At first my aunt refused to acknowledge him, but after some persuasion on my father's part, she agreed to take pity on him.

He stood before her, gazing at a point on the wall slightly above her head. He asked her a brief question about the children and then went into the other room. They did not make up at first and slept in separate beds.

It was too quick, the way in which things returned to normal between them, and it was not to my aunt's liking. Just two days after his homecoming, he started to brood and speak to her in monosyllables. He combed down his hair again so that it tapered to an elegant curl in the middle of his forehead, took up his car keys and, as if a car was being sent for him, walked slowly down the stairs, squaring his shoulders.

We gathered on the two small balconies when my aunt's husband announced that her unmarried brother would be arriving at any moment. Some of us climbed upon the railings, craning our heads round to the right. Every once in a while, my aunt's patience ran out and she left the balcony to go inside. She returned a few moments later. My mother was a little moved by curiosity. She emerged from inside, looked out at the crossroads, then at the street in front of the building, and then went back indoors.

Suddenly the car appeared at the crossroads. My aunt's husband saw it first. In order to make absolutely sure that we knew it was him, my uncle let out two sharp blasts on the horn and waved his long arm out of the car window. It was a white Opel. He parked it at the kerb in front of the building and raced up the stairs.

All my aunt's questions were about the difference between this car and her husband's taxi. It appeared that she knew little about cars when she asked him what colour the interior was and the distance between the front seat and the back seat. My father had just got out of bed. He was sitting on the couch, his eyes swollen, showing no sign of the curiosity that was consuming everyone else in the flat, and when my uncle sat down on the couch near him, he began to ask about the official regulations regarding registration and how much it cost.

My uncle looked tall and slim when he stood before the car and when he stooped to get inside. He had a big feather duster in his hand and waved it in the air, so that it fluffed up big like a peacock's tail. He held it by the top so that the feathers hung down on the surface of the car. He was so tall that he could dust the whole interior of the car without budging from where he stood. He put the duster in the immaculate boot of the car and listened for the rich clunk the lid made when he closed it.

My aunt would sit beside her brother in the front seat, and her children sat with my other aunt in the back. That was the arrangement until after a while he became friendly with one of our village relatives and sat him up front, while my two aunts crowded with the children into the back.

My uncle's idea of a proper outing was a long drive in the car. He took the family to Tripoli, to Baalbek, to the cedars up above Ehden, and the Bekaa valley. In Baalbek, he posed against the background of a wide green field bordered by a stream. Looking slim in his striped grey suit, he walked towards the edge and stared down into the narrow channel and the rapid flow of water, then went back to the middle of the field, back to gazing at his shiny black shoes on the grass.

In Baalbek, he seemed bored, impatient for the time when we would eat. At last my aunt opened the bags into which she had put the containers filled with all kinds of food.

Both my aunts treated their day out as if someone had instructed them how to behave. They sat in the shade of a tree or in a secluded spot near the water. My Aunt Aliya imagined herself in a photograph that showed her sitting under the tree and near the water.

After my uncle had eaten, he rushed them to leave. They replaced the empty, dirty dishes in the bags, and gathered the children together near the car.

After leaving Baalbek behind, on the long, straight road, my aunt began to tease him and ask him questions so that he would not fall asleep. She thought of all kinds of topics, deliberately varying her tone to keep his attention, but when he lost control and the car drifted dangerously close to the roadside, my aunt smacked him on the shoulder and he raised his head, looking dazedly at the tarmac stretching out before him.

At some point after a number of these outings, my father began to ask what was the point of them. He said that my uncle was out running around when he should have been using the time for sleeping, and that he was always groggy at the bakery, not keeping an eye on the workers and uninterested in the customers.

But my uncle grew bored himself with the excursions; otherwise, he would not have paid the least attention to what my father said. Not only had his enthusiasm for the outings ebbed away, he even began to neglect the car. He no longer cared about it being immaculate or finding the best spot to park it in. It was not long before he began to load huge bags of bread in it to deliver to customers' homes.

Now it was easy for my aunt's husband to get the keys away from him. He would be gone in the car for an hour or two, and when he came back he would place the keys on the little table near my sleeping uncle's head, then go out again, but this time in his own taxi.

My uncle had bursts of enthusiasm for things, but always fell into a kind of stupor afterwards. Even his regular coming and going between the bakery and the flat didn't last long. He took to coming and honking the horn for his sister, who would hurry down from the flat to join him. They were not gone long, and when they returned they would finish their conversation on the stairs. He would not leave her alone even in the flat. She told him to go ahead and do something about it, to tell the girl outside her school, to repeat to the girl what he had just said to her.

When she went with him to the school, she was certain that he would not dare to greet the girl in question. He parked the car at the intersection in front of the school. They waited there for her, for a long time, and as soon as the girls began to leave the school he sparked the engine. Then he turned it off. He switched it on again and began to move off hurriedly when he saw the girl coming out of the school gate.

He tried in vain to point out to my aunt which one of the

girls so agitated him. But she could not distinguish between them. All she remembered were the nearly identical navy-blue skirts and blouses with breast pockets, and the silhouette of a blonde teacher whose long straight hair hung down to her waist.

My mother gave birth to my second sister in the heat of summer. But every so often a light breeze blew through the open door of the room. And because she could not bear sitting in bed, she got up and sat on the bare tiles of the floor, resting her back against the closet and folding the child's clothing or sprinkling pine nuts and shelled almonds on creamy desserts she had prepared in cups for the guests.

My mother would say exactly the same thing every time a breeze stirred, as if she were alerting us before it came through the window or dispersed in the dead air of the room. 'There's a breeze,' she would say, and my brother Ali would lift up his head and take a deep breath; but my younger brother just stared at the cups standing in a row before him.

After my sister was born my mother knew my father would now come home much earlier than usual. She stayed in her white nightgown and kept herself occupied with more trivial things than usual. A strong gust tossed the tops of the china bark trees, the noise of the wind filling the room. My mother looked out at the treetops and went over to the bed where my little sister lay. When the breeze died down, she sat closer to the door. She would look out at the high roofs of the buildings and the long line of the horizon on the sea. When her two guests showed up, she sent my brother Ali off to the little grocery shop a good distance from the apartment.

Munira and her mother came in, wearing loose and elegant clothes. Their house was a long way away. They now seldom visited us, but never stopped visiting completely, as if some nostalgia still drove them to come, or they were still hoping for some special occasion to make their coming worthwhile.

Munira was carrying a long rectangular box wrapped in shiny paper. She and her mother sat close to one another on two chairs, and my mother busied herself tentatively before them, getting up and then sitting down; walking towards the door and back again without really doing anything.

Munira and her mother were distant relatives of my mother, and when they sat beside each other there in the room, she felt she was back in the village and that they were sitting on my grandmother's bench.

They allowed my mother to escape from the oppressive atmosphere of the flat. She said that her own relatives had come and so my aunt, my father's sister, had to go into the kitchen or even into her bedroom.

My brother Ali came back from the shop. My mother got up and took the box of chocolates he had brought for the special occasion. Placed before Munira and her mother, the little chocolates wrapped in silver paper were still as cool and fresh as if they had just been taken out of the refrigerator. My mother chatted with the two women, who quietly looked out the open door at the tops of the china bark trees in the heat. They left after exchanging elaborate goodbyes with my mother.

My mother returned to the room after they had gone. She rearranged the chairs and collected the coffee cups, thinking idly of all the cousins Munira had mentioned.

When my mother gave birth, it was also an occasion for my aunt to celebrate. Neighbours and relatives came to offer their congratulations, lingered a little in my mother's room, and then my aunt would gradually lead them away into other rooms, other conversations. She was forever finishing a conversation with Nabiha al-Shibani which they had begun the day before, and conversations with relatives that began in front of my mother went on and on in the kitchen or out on the big balcony.

Umm Ibrahim al-Kilani sat on the floor opposite my mother. She had a pale skin and even teeth, and a light sweat covered her face and neck. The breeze blew and dried her face a little, and then the perspiration reappeared. Her visits had grown more frequent since the early months of my mother's pregnancy. At Umm Ibrahim's insistence, she had even gone down to their flat on the second floor. She would sit with her, chatting a little, and then they would promise to visit one another more often. Umm Ibrahim came up two or three days later. She left her children in the flat, and my mother took none of us with her when she went down to visit a few days later, as if accepting the precedent set by her neighbour on that first visit.

In the al-Kilanis' flat, they would sit in the same room in the same position as in our flat, across from one another before the big open door on to the balcony. My mother's gaze would be drawn to the view of the park and the street as they appeared from the al-Kilanis' flat. From here, the treetops and branches were not visible, only the huge bare trunks.

Umm Ibrahim said that our flat was cooler in summer; that was why she stayed so long when she visited us. She stayed until sundown, and then she would get up quickly and go. My mother would go back into the room after seeing her to the door, and pick up the two coffee cups, casting a quick look at my sister sleeping in her bed.

The disappearance of the red-faced man in the Gordini came as no surprise to Mathilde. Even when he had honked his horn several times she had taken no notice of him. And recently she knew that he would not wait long, so she took her time going out to the balcony.

His absence changed none of her habits. She still spent most of her time alone in the flat, and her quietly impassive features remained the same, never changing as she trod the four steps separating her door from Madame Khayyat's. Nor had anything changed in her relations with the other tenants in the building. She greeted people who greeted her, drily and sharply, never letting go of the metal door handle, as though to signify that she was in a hurry to enter her flat.

My aunt got muddled whenever she encountered her outside her front door. She did not know how to greet her, or whether she should wait for a reply. Sometimes she decided, when she was at the bottom of the stairs leading to the third floor and she knew Mathilde was up there, that she would pass without turning round or acknowledging her. She turned her face a little to the left as she mounted the stairs, her eyes fixed on the wall above her as if following an imaginary line drawn on it, but she got flustered at the last minute and spoke a confused and hasty greeting, then hurried on up the stairs without giving herself a chance to hear the reply.

On one occasion Mathilde definitely did not return the greeting. My aunt was sure of it – there was no room for doubt. She had said nothing, but her swollen eyelids had closed nervously for a moment. She had not returned the greeting. My aunt went up to the flat but did not stay long and went down to see Nabiha al-Shibani, who was at home on her own.

Nabiha al-Shibani aggravated my aunt even more. She would stop my aunt's torrent of irritable gossip to speak of something else. She would jerk her head up and the veins in her neck would swell as she talked interminably away, until my aunt moved quickly towards her own apartment to shut her neighbour up.

Back in her own flat, she muttered in staccato, disconnected bursts. No one else spoke, and she did not direct her complaints at anyone in particular. She would complain about certain classes of people, never naming anybody. My mother put the jigsaw of my aunt's scattered hints together and realized that her target was Mathilde, that woman of uncertain paternity, who had never accepted even a scrap of neighbourly food.

On his daily stroll at the hour of sunset, the Russian man saw nothing different from what he had been seeing for years. The stone wall of the park was the same; nor had the houses facing the wall to the east changed. They still had small gardens at the front, and vines, flowers, and house plants crowded the balconies of the apartments, which served as gardens for the upper storeys. The Russian saw nothing new. The tenants of the houses had not changed, even though they were now fewer in number and rarely strayed far from their front doors.

He stopped and leaned against the stone wall of the park. The inhabitants of this street had not changed much because their gardens had made it impossible to build in the empty spaces. The builders had planned it that way, had deliberately made the sidewalks tremendously wide and left large spaces around the entrances to the ground-level doors. The neighbourhood was neat and orderly, as it had been since he first started taking his walks. It was as silent as it had always been. The building at the end of the street, erected more recently, prevented the traffic noise from reaching these houses.

He had never varied the route of his walk. He was not curious about the changes going on in the south of the city. He walked slowly, and even the sight of a stone that had fallen from the wall would upset him. He did not like the sight of the old statue they had moved from its former site in the town square and re-erected in the lower corner of the park. He noticed it suddenly one evening, and was cross because he had not seen the various stages of its installation on his previous walks.

He could not get away from the smell of the street that surrounded the park. It was stronger at certain times, which he knew well, when the dry, fine-veined fruit of the china bark trees dropped on the ground. He knew how high up in the tree branches the birds settled. And when he went out wearing his old brown hat, he did not lean on the wall or even put his hand on it, because he knew that the rainwater had penetrated deep into the sandstone.

When he was overcome by weariness on his way back, he rested between steps. Once he sat down on the kerbstone in front of a house not far from his own building. He placed his cane by his leg and began to watch the children as if declaring a silent wish to talk with them.

The oldest boy asked him about Russia. They had formed a circle around him; he was in the middle with his cane beside him. He smiled and a cough made his cheeks and chin tremble. He talked about how things used to be when he first came to live here. He talked about people while pointing to the apartments in which they lived. He coughed in the middle of his sentences, and his eyebrows knitted together, reminding the children of his angry moments and of the times when he looked agitated on his promenade.

When he began to rise, one of the children clasped his arm. He did not seem to want to be led by them from this place of rest to his own house. He walked slowly, though never stopping to lean against the walls or doors of the shops.

Since the day the rumour spread among the children that the Russian's daughter trained as a boxer, I heard, whenever I passed by the window of their flat, the sound of punches on the bag that hung from the ceiling over bare tiles. I imagined her standing in front of the bag in the austere room, with all kinds of athletic equipment around her, along the walls and in the corners.

The Russian's plump blonde daughter never spoke. When she put her firm feet on the ground, the children ran to look at her hair, which she braided like a pretzel. She looked like a little girl trapped in a big womanly body.

She married an Englishman. He stayed in their flat for two days, and when he left he was carrying her suitcases – he refused to let her carry anything. My aunt saw him from the fifth floor. He was young with a short beard, and worked as a dentist in his own country.

The old Russian, who wanted to carry out the proper farewell ritual, insisted on accompanying them out as far as the car door, but as the boot was being closed on the suitcases he was still making his way down the three steps, leaning against the iron railing. He had not quite descended the last step when the car sped away.

Her mother was at the window. When the car drove away with them in it, she closed the windows as if there was some household task she urgently needed to do. My aunt said we should go to their flat and console them. Her husband began to joke when he heard her say this, and told my father, who was sitting beside him, that my aunt loved to practise her French with the Russians, and he laughed to himself at the thought of his wife composing her features into those of a French-speaker. My mother said that Nabiha al-Shibani and Madame Laure had put it into her head because they had already been down to the Russians' flat with their husbands on the evening of the day their daughter left.

There were three loudspeakers hanging from the wide chimney that rose several metres from the roof, aimed in different directions, pointing towards the nearby buildings and the street that led to the al-Munla district.

All day long the bustle in our flat grew busier, working towards a climax. Our relatives came from the village – my grandfather and grandmother and anyone who was even remotely related to us. So did our Beiruti relatives, even the ones who lived on the periphery of the city. They had all been invited, as had everyone who had the slightest connection with anyone in the flat. My father told me to invite the teachers from my school. I waited for them at the park gate because they did not know this part of Beirut very well. They all showed up, and on the short walk back to the flat they asked me whether my uncle was an educated man.

It was my father's idea to have the party on the roof. He said that there was enough room for all the guests. The bride's family seemed like real Beirutis, because they had moved to the city from the South a long time ago, and their accents were exactly like those of city people in their neighbourhood. The bride was rather tall and spoke rather grandly, and when we saw her a few days before the wedding my brother Ali said she looked like a teacher in a Christian school.

An endless stream of things was brought up to the flat – the place was overflowing. My mother and aunt, my Aunt Aliya and my grandmother and the rest of our female relatives had spent three days cooking and getting things ready so that they would be free on the day of the wedding. My father's and uncle's friends came from the village and from various parts of Beirut, and had been coming up to the roof since the afternoon, telling jokes and stories and laughing.

They had invited our neighbours, from the building and from the whole neighbourhood. The shopkeeper, from the al-Ghazzawi family, seemed quite a different man at the wedding. He was overdressed, and looked like a big flash greengrocer.

The staircase, all five flights, all the way up to the roof, was saturated with brilliant light. My aunt's husband had run a long electrical wire down the well between the flights of stairs, with dozens of bulbs attached to it. My uncle was going up and down the stairs, until just before the party, busily shepherding our female relatives, delivering party supplies, and everything else. When he came upstairs for the last time, his hair was combed and he was clean-shaven; he had put on his striped summer suit after his bath and he was fragrant with cologne.

Nabiha al-Shibani was also preoccupied, after her fashion. She stood facing my mother, aunt, and the other female relatives gathered in the kitchen, telling her endless little jokes. Every once in a while she would ask my aunt whether she didn't need her to go and get something from her flat. On the day of the wedding, all the al-Shibanis' dishes were at our place, and Madame Laure had also loaned us her plates, glasses, and coffee cups.

At one side of the roof, in the corner, my father had hidden a crate filled with bottles of whisky and wine for those who had acquired the habit of drinking in Beirut. My aunt's husband had taken aside all the early arrivals and lifted up the edge of the cover a little, provoking nervous cackles of laughter. One of our male relatives was acting as if he was blind drunk, though he had not yet tasted his first glass.

When the traditional singers began to shake their tambourines, the roof was packed with guests who crowded around them, while knots of people were gathered in the four corners. One of the singers, who knew my father, began to declaim about the generosity of our family for long generations past. Her voice rippled out of the three loudspeakers and reverberated off the walls of the neighbouring buildings and into the street to the south. The people standing at the edge of the roof heard the booming of the loudspeakers instead of her actual voice.

Our relatives repeated like a chorus the singer's words about the honour of the family. Some put their heads together to utter the words, some raised their heads while murmuring the words, and some repeated the words at the top of their voices.

Nabiha al-Shibani was the most excitable of the neighbours. She stood close to the singers and loudly told funny anecdotes to my aunt's husband. She was always the one who introduced groups of people who had nothing in common. Even my schoolteachers, who had gathered in a circle in a corner, smiled only at her.

Madame Laure and her husband stood alone in the space that separated our relatives from the clusters of people in the corners. They would move closer to the table whenever my father or aunt passed by, and retreated again when they weren't around. A cool, absentminded smile never left Madame Laure's husband Abraham's face. It widened on his lips whenever he saw someone looking at him, and the big basket of flowers that carried his and his wife's names stood on the floor between the raised legs of the table.

When the two singers, who were sisters, came forward to the microphone, a murmur ran through the assembly. It was said that my aunt's husband was the one who had invited them. These chanteuses wore elegant backless dresses, and when they stood at the microphone, they started to sing together in unison, their voices echoing from the three loudspeakers, just like the voices of singers on the radio.

My aunt's husband sang some of the words of the song along with them. He was in the front row. Behind him stood a woman who was wiping away the tears that streamed down her cheeks; according to my aunt's husband, she was the singers' mother. One of our relatives said that she was crying at seeing them singing in front of strangers; another said she was crying for joy.

My aunt and mother were discussing opening the boxes and passing round the wedding gifts to the guests. The three boxes in the living room had been brought up by the porters sent by the store that supplied the gifts. My mother had given them food and my father money before their unhurried departure down the stairs.

My mother asked when the gifts should be passed around. She kept on asking this question and did not stop until some of the men carried two of the three big boxes up to the roof and placed them in the corner where al-Ghazzawi the green-grocer was standing. The chaotic distribution began, though there were not enough for everyone as some people took two or three gifts, or even more. My father said that my uncle's wedding had cost thousands of pounds and that my uncle had had to go out three times to the bank in one day to get more money.

As the bride was given away by her father, the two girls sang her a song and she swayed along to the rhythm. Some of our relatives and the other guests, who had forgotten about her minutes after arriving, sang along. My uncle stood beside her, his palm placed carefully inside the jacket of his suit. The dazzling camera light flashed when my father and grand-father stood beside them; then the camera went on to photograph every imaginable combination of people that gathered in front of it.

My father told me to ask my teachers whether they would like to have their picture taken. They stood smiling in a single line in front of the camera, and in the second picture I was with them, standing exactly in the middle.

The photographer was very quiet and compliant even when the guests drank too much and made him take silly pictures of them. He even remained silent when my aunt's husband claimed that he was not really taking their pictures, just flashing lights at them.

When a knot of guests left the spot where they had been standing and went home, the floor beneath them was littered with the shells of pistachios and sunflower seeds and bits of food that stuck to the ground. My mother said that cleaning up after them would take more time than preparing for the wedding. My teachers left without saying all their goodbyes because my father had got drunk and fallen asleep on the bed my mother had put in a room well away from the guests.

Madame Laure and her husband left after he kept insisting they go. They went silently down the stairs to their flat, walking close to one another as though they lived a long way away.

Mathilde paid little attention when Madame Khayyat tried to convince her to go to the wedding like all the other neighbours. She would not even believe that her neighbour had seriously meant what she said. Madame Khayyat was unable to go up to the roof by herself. She stayed at home, like Mathilde, who had lived for days in fear of the racket caused by the crowds of people going up and down the stairs, and the workers carrying chairs and plates and decorations.

The house had never seen such excitement, and Mathilde too almost believed that our flat had expanded and taken over the five flights of stairs and the roof. On the day of the party no one heard the sound of the loudspeakers as acutely as Mathilde. She could not sleep. She sat up in her bed, her legs straight out in front of her, her back rigid against the bedstead.

Madame Khayyat was upset and anxious as well. Mathilde had to wait for her neighbour to come from the back room to let her in. She sat down on the boudoir chair as she always did and they chatted a little. When Mathilde looked across to the side her gaze fell on her neighbour's suitcase which had been taken down from the top of the wardrobe. Madame Khayyat told her that she missed her daughter and her children, and this time she would go up to the mountain and persuade them to come and live with her in her spacious apartment.

She left two days later. The driver carried down the suitcase, which Madame Khayyat had crammed full of clothes.

She locked the door. Her face glistened with the layers of make-up she had applied. Mathilde said goodbye to her. She stood at the railing of the stairway, and watched her go down, stepping back only when Madame Khayyat disappeared into the lower floors of the house.

Part Two

My mother told us to give our keys to my aunt before we left. My brother Ali took my key from me and placed it on his palm alongside his own key, then handed them to my aunt who hesitated slightly before taking them.

After she had taken them, Ali ground his teeth, frowned, and pulled a long face. He bent over the chest on the floor, picked it up, and took it out on to the landing. The two removal men panted as they mounted the final steps to our flat, staggering around and tripping. They took the chest, and one of them tied a rope around it, looping it round his waist and head. Then he put his foot on the top step, while his companion walked cautiously, nimbly, behind him, constantly giving directions.

When the men removed the dresser from its place in the bedroom a thick layer of heavy dust was revealed in the space where it had stood. My aunt hurried to get her broom and began ostentatiously to sweep the dust from the vacant spot. She did the same thing when we moved the gas oven, sweeping the dust that had accumulated underneath it, and then moving her own oven to the middle of the kitchen. By the time my brother had finished moving the big sofa in the living room, she had spread out her sofas around a wider area. She set the little parlour tables farther apart, and brought fresh embroidered tablecloths from her closet for the tables.

My brother Ali got up in the truck with the driver and the removal men. We – my mother, my younger brother, my sisters, and I – walked to the al-Munla quarter. We reached the intersection. My mother turned left while my older sister lugged the heavy bags, though without grumbling. My younger sister carried a bulging bag with both hands, and my younger brother's head was spinning with the things my mother had said about my aunt.

She was being forced to leave the flat, she had said. My father had not invoked his right to occupy the apartment, his right to something that was his father's property. The deed was in our grandfather's name – how could my father have kept quiet and said nothing?

My aunt had rearranged the room right in front of us, as if we were guests who had stayed a little too long. She had come to the flat three months earlier than we had, with my grandfather, Wasila, and Umm Habib. In spite of the long years of our residence she still thought, because of those three months she had on us, that we were interfering where we had no business when any of us suggested putting curtains around the exposed storage space or closing the door of the Arab-style bathroom because the water ran over and streamed out of the door into the hallway.

The night before we left, I could not look my aunt's husband in the eye. He didn't say a word, and his eyebrows were knitted together, just waiting for one of us to say something. My father did not speak to him when he came back from the bakery and found him sitting on the big sofa in the living room, looking coolly around the room as though he now owned it. When my father came into the room where we were sitting, he did not want to eat. He said he was tired. My mother set out a mattress for him, and he fell asleep as soon as he laid his head on the pillow.

My mother turned into a street that led uphill. The road seemed very long as we looked up from where we stood to where it came to an end. My mother suggested that we rest a little. We stopped and put our bags on the ground. My mother leaned against a wall and my younger sister rubbed her palms together to get rid of the red marks the handle of the bag had dug into her flesh. When we began walking again, my mother abandoned her position at the front of the group. Her steps were so short that she seemed to be going backwards. Seeing her on the road like that made me feel as if I was seeing her walk for the first time. I was surprised at how close she kept to the houses and the way she crossed the streets. By the time we crossed the al-Munla district and reached the places I used to go with other children, I was looking at her as though she were a different woman.

It saddened her that we were leaving the flat after all those years. When Nabiha al-Shibani and Madame Laure came up to say goodbye, they had not stayed very long. But Nabiha al-Shibani let herself be drawn in by my aunt's prattling about the rearrangement of the furniture in the rooms and the redecoration of the living room. They said goodbye to my mother as if this were the end of one of their ordinary visits when my mother had been ill or had had a baby. Madame Laure did not linger; she said she had something on the stove and was afraid it would burn.

When we reached the second floor, Umm Ibrahim al-Kilani suddenly opened the door, as if she had been able to see right through it and knew that we had reached her landing. She hugged my mother, tears glistening in her eyes; my mother was crying as well, but her tears were choked back, constricting her throat. Saying goodbye to Umm Ibrahim, her voice was low and shaky, with a very strange tone to it.

Umm Ibrahim al-Kilani had a dull face, and it had never looked duller than now. She stood there completely still, her hand resting on the balustrade until we walked out of the building entrance and reached the street.

My mother's steps grew smaller the higher we climbed the steep street to the petrol station. Her short legs seemed to move nimbly, as she took more steps, but she was barely moving forward. My younger brother told me jokingly that we would have to push her if we wanted to get as far as the petrol station.

We had rested on the steps. My father, having made it down the four flights of stairs, was pale and panting for breath as if his heart were about to stop. We knew that as he reached the second floor he'd begun to have one of his usual coughing fits. He leaned on the railing or the wall and paused before throwing away his cigarette.

My mother said that the new house was not far from the petrol station. A few more steps and we'd be there. The street was crowded, and both sides were crammed with shops selling cooking oil and vegetables, a butcher's shop, a pharmacy, two cinemas side by side, a barber-shop, and a restaurant. The owner of the grocery shop opposite our new flat hurried out to greet us. He was from a village near ours. He knew our grandfather, he said, and some of our close relatives.

The two removal men had put all the furniture they'd brought down inside the front door of the new house. When we entered the black cast-iron gate, the landlord came down from his apartment on the second floor, wearing the kind of white hat that old village men wore in the South. He greeted my mother without shaking her hand, the proper greeting for a Shiite woman, and led us through the rooms of our new apartment, keeping up as he went a patter of words of welcome, proverbs, and pious maxims.

When I went back to see the big park, the street that ran along the wall had a different smell. I thought at first that it was the smell of the little fruit of the china bark tree, with its dry fuzzy bloom. The fruit had a gluey, gummy resin that stuck to your fingers and clothes, but you could smell it from a distance when the fruit dried out and became desiccated. But this was not the same old smell; it came from somewhere else.

I went into the park. The green wooden benches had been replaced by marble ones whose cold penetrated my back as soon as I sat down. I got up and walked towards the patches of sunlight, to the clearings among the trees. The trees were far

96

sparser. On the north side the dense flowering trees had been torn up and replaced by orderly flower beds and a narrow concrete path. Now that part of the park was nothing more than a passage for getting to the other side. Before, it had resembled a little jungle. I walked round the side of the park. I rested under the weak sun, on a marble bench. I opened my book to finish reading where I had left off the day before.

The building looked taller than I had remembered, and it seemed, from that distance, to have preserved the straightness and angular delicacy of its proportions. It still looked new, in this light. The little balconies, all level and parallel with each other, made me notice that the broad wall of the building was still clean, even bright, from some vantage points, as if the painter had just completed his last brushstroke. From the point where I sat in the park, the house looked so tall that it seemed to stand alone, to stand apart from the buildings surrounding it.

The Russian man was the only one who had ever seen the building standing alone among vacant lots. To him the corners of the wall had seemed even until he looked closely and felt them with his hand. His white face alive with movement and his smooth brown hair falling slightly over his forehead, the Russian man was the only person who could have smelled the new paint and felt with his hand the shiny metal of the new faucets. Everything in the building gleamed when as a young man he had entered his apartment on the ground floor. Not concerned about the arrival of other tenants in the building, he had spent his time looking at the people walking in the park. Maybe he might become friendly with some of them.

The building still looked new when you looked at it from

the park and from a certain distance. You would have thought it had only aged on the inside, that only the steps, railings and balconies were worn out. But it had also aged on the side that didn't face the park, the side with the big balconies and on which there were heavy water pipes running up to the roof. The big balconies were the flats' open-air storehouses: my aunt put all her plants out there, Madame Laure spread her drying laundry over her balcony, and Umm Ibrahim al-Kilani had an ancient refrigerator in the corner of hers.

The big balconies overlooked the crowded poorer streets, and were the most dilapidated part of the building. The tenants made no attempt to keep up appearances on that side. But people would show themselves off on the small balconies at the front, after dressing up carefully, as though they were paying visits. My aunt would look out from the wooden door, walk out to the railing, and look down, then go back indoors and close the door.

When I went up the stairs, no one opened their door. The old glass cover still shielded the light over Mathilde's door. Madame Laure was still redecorating her flat, as usual. Her door looked glossy, as though its paint were fresh and wet. I pressed my aunt's bell. I heard her rapid footsteps on the tile hallway before she opened the door.

Outside on the big balcony she told me that she had sensed that I was coming to see her. She spoke of my father's estrangement and repeated some things she had heard that my mother had been saying about her. She was the only one left in the flat.

The kitchen seemed enormous, bare. She had put dinner plates on the table in the corner. The flat was clean and tranquil. Madame Laure was coming up shortly, she said. I delighted in the way she treated me like a grown man when she brought me a cup of coffee on a saucer. She placed it on a little table, sat across from me, and began to ask about our new flat and about which of our relatives visited us, while sipping her coffee down to the grounds in the bottom of the cup.

Madame Laure seemed much more at ease than me in the flat. As soon as she came in she started talking loudly – I could hear her from where I sat out on the big balcony. My aunt announced that I had come, and she then came out to greet me elaborately and ask about my mother. I told her I had noticed the new coat of paint on her door. She had replaced her glasses with a pair with thicker lenses. And she was carrying a pair of knitting needles and a ball of yarn.

The consecutive movements of her hands gave me a sense of the intimacy that connected her to my aunt. Behind them was the wall of the neighbouring building. The doorway was filled with warm sunlight that lit the room inside. Madame Laure did not stay long. I assume that it was my presence that inclined her to leave. My aunt asked me if I was hungry. I got up from the balcony and went into the sitting room. It was roomy but dark and dull. My aunt had bought new highbacked sofas and there was now a cornice of brown-painted plaster. The room adjoining the sitting room was empty and my aunt had not covered the bare tile floor. The walls were high and cold, and only a thin curtain covered the door to the balcony. I pulled the curtain aside; through the locked glass door I could look out across the park to where I had just been walking and from where I had gazed across at the building.

Nabiha al-Shibani did not know whether she had been awakened by his first cries or whether she had slept on as he called for help. His voice sounded as though it were coming from underneath the blanket: weak and muffled, but insistent. When she turned on the light, she saw him, and his appearance was frightening. Sweat poured off him, and his cheeks were ashen.

She did not know what to do. She rushed to where the children were sleeping, but when she reached the hallway between the bedrooms his voice – now even weaker and more strangled – pulled her back. She did not know what to do, and spent a few crucial moments hesitating back and forth between his room and the children's rooms.

When my aunt opened the door to her, she was trembling and pacing to and fro on the small landing. She told my aunt that her husband had died, and went back downstairs without waiting for her, while my aunt rushed back inside to wake up her husband and pull a dress over her head.

When my aunt got downstairs, Nabil was against the wall, clinging to it, as if someone was pushing him to where his father lay and he was resisting. His eyes were wide and staring, and he was trembling like his mother, but he did calm down. When my aunt approached him he told her the same thing his mother had told her. He said that his father was dead, and watched her as she went over to his sisters, who were cowering close to one another.

When Madame Laure came in the evidence of rudely broken sleep was plain upon her face. She fought a trembling that had come upon her the moment she left her warm bed. She patted the children on the shoulders and constantly switched her attention between the two girls and their mother. She spoke to each girl alone in a soft whisper, and when she poked her head round the door to see where Said al-Shibani lay, Nabil took a step backwards while Nabiha al-Shibani let out a scream that made both of her daughters burst into tears at the same instant.

He lay stretched out in the room, his face still reflecting his struggle against death. The blanket was in a heap at his feet. His wife had done nothing to change his position, and though she knew she should cover him she had not pulled up the rumpled blanket. She was afraid, and left all that for the other tenants in the building to do.

My aunt's husband went to Nabil, whose eyes were still wide. He shook his hand and told him that now, and from now on, he was the man of the family. He spoke these words without a trace of emotion, and when he was finished he went into the parlour, sat down on the sofa, and started smoking cigarette after cigarette.

Madame Laure said that there was nothing anyone could do before morning. Her husband came in. He was clean-shaven and wearing a grey suit. He sat by my aunt's husband in the parlour and they began talking about the last few times they had met Said al-Shibani on the stairs.

It occurred to my aunt's husband that the tenants of the building were like a single family as he watched my aunt serve coffee to everyone sitting in the flat. Before that she had made the beds and tidied the sitting room. After hastily straightening up the other rooms, she went into the parlour. She put ashtrays on the tables and placed more chairs in the empty areas between the sofas. She was preparing the flat for all those who would come in the morning.

Mathilde waited until seven o'clock in the morning before coming. Madame Laure had broken the news to her about two hours before that. She made her way slowly to Nabiha al-Shibani and spoke briefly to her and also to her daughters. She spoke a few words of comfort to Nabil from a few steps away. Her rough voice made the girls stop crying. She had done her duty and now went into the parlour and sat on the sofa facing Madame Laure's husband. She laced her hands together on her chest and fell silent.

In the morning, Said al-Shibani's relatives came from their district, which was on the other side of Beirut, to the east. The way they climbed the stairs, it was impossible to tell whether they were in a hurry, or taking their time. But one of them put his hand on the railing and came up two steps at a time, jumping as though expecting a surprise, then slowing down and waiting for the others coming up behind him.

My aunt had heard about them but never met them before. His brother looked nothing like Said al-Shibani, though he dressed like the dead man. Al-Shibani had had many acquaintances, though in his flat and on the stairs he never gave any hint of it. The visitors now came into the flat so quietly that no one in the kitchen could have known that the parlour was crowded with them.

My aunt went frequently into the parlour to empty the ashtrays that filled up so quickly. There was not the slightest doubt in her mind that he had died from the amount of arak he had drunk before going to bed. The bottle on the sink was empty, and in the room where he lay the air was heavy with the same smell she had become used to on her many visits to their flat.

My aunt did the housework and received the guests with such easy graciousness that it made Madame Laure think she must have been used to such occasions. Even in the crowd of guests she managed not to ignore Nabil and his sisters and would ask them every now and then whether they were hungry. She prepared them some food, set it out on the table, and insisted that they eat. They went into the kitchen with her. Nabil ate first, without appetite to begin with, and his sisters followed. They had begun to talk among themselves when they heard Nabiha al-Shibani shriek at the sight of her husband, who had been dressed up in his black suit and shiny shoes. Nabil dropped the mouthful of food he had been about to eat into the saucer of his teacup. His sisters left their cups on the table and ran to their mother. Said was outstretched, his forearms crossed over his chest. The girls began to sob, and the neighbours tried in vain to make them go back into the kitchen or out on to the big balcony.

All the tenants in the building came to the al-Shibani flat except the Russians whose absence no one noticed. Umm Ibrahim al-Kilani did not stay long. She hesitated over where to sit and, to hide her confusion, she walked behind my aunt, following her from room to room. When she came to offer condolences to Nabiha al-Shibani, she delivered herself of a great many solemn proverbs and sayings appropriate to the occasion. My aunt was touched by the feeling of warm solidarity among the tenants of the building as she imagined how Umm Ibrahim's tone must have sounded in Nabiha al-Shibani's ears.

The coffin they carried into the room was black and gleaming, decorated with fittings in gold-plated metal. There was a sudden eruption of sobbing and crying as it was brought in through the door, and it grew louder and fiercer when the men lifted the corpse and placed it inside, on the shiny, quilted violet cloth. According to my aunt the body had slid into the coffin in one go, without even an elbow striking the edge.

The big black hearse waited at the entrance to the building. My aunt wondered aloud how the people who had sent wreaths of flowers had prepared them so quickly. Bouquets continued to arrive even after the last leavetakers had gone down to the entrance. I watched the coffin through the railings as they carried it down the stairs. Nabiha al-Shibani and her daughters accompanied it. Nabil walked behind it, escorted by a male cousin on one side and Madame Laure's husband on the other.

The people walked along behind the infinitely slow-moving hearse. Nabiha al-Shibani and her daughters were in the lead, dressed in black. Nabil was crying, staring at a fixed point on the back of the great vehicle. My aunt's husband was with them, and before the hearse took a right turn, he looked up at the balcony of his flat to see whether my aunt had seen him there among the mourners. She was there; Mathilde, too, was on her balcony, and Umm Ibrahim al-Kilani, with her son and her waif-like daughter, was looking down from their balcony on the second floor.

The walls of the stairway and the black railings, the doors to the flats and the large fanlights did not give the same impression of the building as when it was seen from the outside, from that exact spot in the park. The thick green door in my aunt's flat, the one that led from the kitchen to the big balcony, was cracked from the bottom, and its many coats of paint made it hard to close. When I looked at the façade of the building from that vantage point, all I could see was the sharp outline of its elevation; all I could see of the balconies was their parallel railings. From there you could not see the gaps in the yellow paint here and there, or the cracks in the bottom of the al-Kilanis' balcony. The building looked exactly as it would in an architect's plan: all straight lines and colours, balconies and windows as if drawn on paper.

From inside, the building looked very different, especially the first two floors where the tops of the walls, near the ceilings, showed just how many times the entrance and hallways had been painted. A high crumbly patch with a layer of peeling paint showed the many successive colours of the wall.

When I went to visit my aunt a second time after we had left the flat, I noticed that the coloured glass panes had fallen out of the electric lights above all the doorways except those of Mathilde and Madame Laure. The texture of the glass was wavy, as if wrapped in tissue, and in the middle of each pane was a pink floral device enclosed in twin blue circles. My aunt had installed a light over her door which, when turned on, lit her floor and the floor below, and part-lit the edges of the floors adjoining the stairwell all the way down.

This time, too, I did not see a single one of the tenants on the stairs. The doors were locked, just as they had been on my last visit. On the fourth floor, passing the al-Shibani flat, I recalled the noise people had made as the black coffin was carried down. I guessed that Said al-Shibani's death had had the effect of inhibiting people's habit of lingering on the stairs.

My aunt's certainty about his cause of death was shared by Madame Laure, whom she visited constantly. He had died from drinking too much arak the night of his death. He had not been complaining of anything, and might have lived for years if it were not for his alcoholism, which he had made no effort to control.

Madame Laure passed this on to Mathilde, and when my aunt talked to Umm Ibrahim al-Kilani on the stairs, she spoke eloquently on the subject of sin, the prohibitions of religion and the evils of drink.

My aunt's theory was gradually accepted throughout the building. Even Nabiha al-Shibani endorsed it, though the morning after his death she said that he had drunk no more than usual because he had gone to bed early. The idea spread through all the flats in the building, and by the time Umm Ibrahim heard it for the second time, it was being said that Said al-Shibani had only ever been able to get any colour into his ghastly cheeks by slapping them.

Madame Laure finished up her chores quickly as soon as her husband had left for work so that she could hurry to my aunt's flat. Mathilde went to see her twice but did not find her in. She knew that she was at my aunt's but something prevented her from going up to the fifth floor. Madame Khayyat had postponed her return from the mountain this time. The last few times she had always come back down to Beirut in the company of her daughter's family. They came into the flat, dusted off the tables, chairs, and cabinets, slept there for a night or two, then went back to the mountains.

Even in the two days she spent at home she never left the children. Mathilde saw very little of her, and even then she would be sitting in the parlour with the children, who filled the room with their noise and shouting. Their presence prevented Mathilde from overcoming her silence and speaking in her measured way, pausing between each word she spoke. Madame Khayyat would get up and walk her to her flat and wait until she had locked her door and her footsteps could be heard receding down her hallway.

My aunt said that Nabiha al-Shibani knew why her husband had called to her in his low, strangulated voice. He knew that he was dying. He had made that great effort to wake her up and she had not heard him, even though her bed was right beside his. He had struggled in his last moments to tell her where he had put his money. Nabiha al-Shibani told her that as she trembled and ran in the direction of the children's rooms, he had shaken his head and motioned with his hand for her to come near.

It was only a slight movement of the hand, but it was all he could manage. Nabiha al-Shibani was lost. She did not know what to do, and her husband had died with agony in his heart because he had been unable to utter a last word to his wife.

My aunt said that she did not rule out the possibility that the al-Shibanis were now in need, barely having enough money for their food and other expenses. She also said that she wouldn't be surprised if this explained the long stay at their relatives' house.

Nabiha al-Shibani and her children did spend a considerable time with their relatives. Madame Laure had heard that while there the older daughter Katya had got married to a neighbour of the relatives. She had gone ahead and married him before the mourning period was over, and now lived with him in a house in that district.

When Madame Laure stood on her rear balcony and looked down, she could see the date trees, the watchman's house and the dry pool. All she now remembered of the watchman who had left after such a short time were his face and the sight of his bald head. Before he left, the tenants had wondered what he was doing for the building. All he had to do was to safeguard the key to the roof and wait for the season to pick the dates. One morning the tenants had seen him go out with a porter's rope over his shoulder; he did not come back that evening.

Madame Laure still remembered the garden he had created in front of his tiny house. The tin pots of varying sizes were spread over an area larger than the area of the hut. He had planted flowers, vegetables, and even small trees. Madame Laure remembered the slow desiccation that afflicted the plants after the watchman had gone. In time, nothing was left but a cactus root and a small tree stump which sprouted a few blossoms for part of the year.

The dilapidated house looked very different now. The border between the garden and the empty lot had disappeared. As time went on there was no sign of even the cactus root and the small tree stump, and even the tin pots seemed to be disintegrating. Nothing to speak of was left of the garden, even though Madame Laure was still able, without great effort, to redraw in her mind the lines that separated the garden from the empty lot.

She was helped in this by the position of the watchman's hut, from which she could trace the imaginary borders. The house, neglected for all those years, looked as though it were slowly drowning in sand. She couldn't imagine that it was even possible to venture inside now: the effect of merely stepping in might cause the roof to collapse. It was made of temporary materials: sheets of zinc, wood, and lengths of cloth taken from an old tent. In order to stabilize the roofing materials, the builder had positioned stones at the corners and in the middle.

When Madame Laure noticed the children in the lot, she thought they must have come in from the street and climbed over the locked iron gate. But she then noticed that the door of the house was open. A man of about fifty came out, bent over, clasped the lower part of the door with both hands, and shoved it up in an effort to make it level. Once shut, he locked it with a padlock he had on him. He walked away and the

111

children followed him; Madame Laure rushed up to see my aunt.

In the days that followed, the man began to repair the house. The children helped him, handing him the stones and planks that he put on the roof. Once it was ready to be lived in, the man began to move in old furniture. His wife seemed strong as she carried in closet doors and lifted down a thick wooden table balanced on her head.

When the tenants began to trade gossip about what they saw, they referred to him ironically as their 'new neighbour'. Madame Laure went out on to my aunt's balcony to monitor the movements of the man and his children as they came in and out of the shack.

He seemed just like anyone else. Madame Laure said that he acted as though he'd lived there for a long time, as though he were a real tenant. Guests from the nearby al-Munla district visited him every evening. They sat on little chairs and chatted until it was night, and then left after the man had put out a big lamp to light the dirt path.

Madame Laure was astonished at the number of people who lived in the little house. Seeing the shoes piled up outside the door made her think they must be sleeping in the kitchen and even in the bath. Nor was the house restricted to the large family, for men she had never seen before often emerged in the morning. It was as if they came there to sleep for a single night and then left, never to return.

No one in the family ever looked up at the big balconies. When the children played in the vacant lot, their faces were permanently turned the other way, towards the stone wall that separated the building from the al-Munla quarter. Madame Laure told my aunt that when they did face the building they took care to keep their faces cast down. If they wanted to look up at something, they raised only their eyes, with their heads lowered.

When the men sat around in the evening they recounted what they had done during the day. The circle formed by their little chairs was irregular; very few men sat facing the building. Madame Laure said that they were very close to the Russians' flat, whose rear balcony looked out on the empty lot. She said that they would startle the old woman when she went into her kitchen, which they could see into. Madame Laure said this, not knowing that the Russians had in fact shut the wooden door that opened on to the lot. They rarely even opened the window. The Russian lady had locked it long ago, having heard the voices outside and having wondered for some time who they belonged to before discovering that they were new neighbours.

They filled the space down there with movement from early in the morning until late at night. In the daytime, the woman did many of her chores outside. She put the big canister of gas near the door while leaving the long-necked bottle inside. She took a wooden stick and stirred her laundry as she boiled it in a barrel. In the afternoon, when she had finished, the people up on their balconies would see the large load of laundry she had washed: there were so many clothes that there was not even enough room for them laid out on the sides of the pool and on the long stone wall.

My aunt and Madame Laure guessed at how much rent the landlord was charging the family for the watchman's house. He was a miser, my aunt said. She wouldn't be surprised to see him start renting out the empty landings in the building. Madame Laure subsequently saw Umm Ibrahim al-Kilani

chatting with the woman while she was going about her out-
door chores. The two women began to talk so often that with
time Umm Ibrahim never left her balcony until she had
exchanged a few words with her neighbour on the sandy
plot. Madame Laure supposed that the relationship between
them would grow closer, but that a certain distance would be
maintained; that they would not visit each other.

When Nabiha al-Shibani came back from the home of her husband's relatives, she was so gaunt that the veins in her neck stood out even when she was not speaking. Madame Laure was unable to chat with her the way she had in the past, and for my aunt it was like visiting a strange new neighbour.

When Samia came into the room, my aunt's suspicion that they were suffering financially was confirmed. The buttons of Samia's black woollen jumper were done up, and her thin stockings were laddered and loose, showing that she too had lost weight.

They guessed that Nabiha al-Shibani would not get back to normal until she ventured out of her flat. Then she went up to see my aunt. As soon as the door was opened, as soon as Nabiha al-Shibani had set foot in the place, the whole flat was overwhelmed with the sound of voices. They sat in the parlour and gradually got her to talk about her husband's relatives' house and her daughter's husband and her son Nabil, whose patience had run out: he could not bear living there any longer.

When she began to talk about her financial troubles she did so without distress. She said that she could not take care of Nabil's needs, which were exorbitant. She spoke without any embarrassment, as if it were a matter of a small cash shortage, or of waiting for the bank to open.

She gave some approximate sense of the fortune her husband had left her, and her estimates of this fortune mounted with every passing day. When Samia went to teach in a private school, the figure went higher than ever before. Samia went down the stairs early, a bulging satchel of sandwiches and small books in her hand. She returned home by evening or a little before, and stopped to gossip with my aunt and Madame Laure about the building and the neighbours.

My aunt couldn't decide whether Samia was beautiful. When she looked at her long blonde hair, she thought back to the evenings when the girl would come out of her bedroom and watch the older women as they sat and talked in the parlour. But when Samia laughed my aunt noticed her prominent gums, which were almost blue, and decided that she was not attractive to men. As she stood in the light, one noticed her fair complexion, which had begun to dry out with the passage of time – so much so that my aunt thought that if she rubbed her cheek with her hand, dry flakes of skin would come off.

Nabiha al-Shibani had not changed her mind about the

fortune she had coming. She fancied that the situation, with Samia working and Nabil living at home, was temporary and would be over once she got the letter from the lawyer who lived abroad. But while always talking about the lawyer's delays, she began to show an exaggerated concern every time my aunt came to visit. She was always commenting on a dress or meal or new shoes. My aunt told Madame Laure that vegetables wilted as soon as they were brought into the al-Shibani flat, and that their food looked as if it had been sitting on the plates for days.

Nabil loved the food prepared in the restaurant just on the outskirts of the al-Munla quarter. A boy would come from the restaurant balancing a platter on his palm. Nabil would take it from him and give him back the platter from the day before.

His mother said nothing to him about his staying on in the flat. She told my aunt that he no longer wanted to go out with the friends he had known since childhood. He sat at home, and when he ran out of the thick paper sheets he used for drawing plans for buildings on the sea front, his mother would go out to buy him more paper from the stationer across the park.

Nabiha al-Shibani gradually stopped talking about the family fortune. On one occasion the owner of the restaurant raised his voice outside her door, shouting that he would not stand for any more delays with payment. Some people in the building heard him. The next morning, a driver with a little truck came and climbed up to their flat, and the removal man was with him. My aunt heard the noise and watched over her railing. Their black piano, still highly polished, stood there in the hot sun, and the driver and removal man looked very wary as they carried it down the steps at the entrance to the building.

Nabiha's daughter Katya used to remember it a few times a year and sit on the round chair and lift the piano's shining cover. She would drum her fingers on it and melodies would fill the whole house and escape beyond its narrow walls.

In the days after the piano had been sold, Nabil started to leave the house, first to go to the nearby stationery store, then further afield. Once he got used to going out, he began to stay out all day, coming home very late. He would go down the stairs slowly, his head held high, toying with his key ring, as if to show that he was going out to his car parked in front of the entrance. Madame Laure said that he was going to travel to Switzerland soon, to meet up with the lawyer.

When the removal man carried down the two Persian rugs from the parlour, Nabil was standing outside the door in quiet conversation with another man who had been brought along. Standing tall, his head raised, Nabil gave the impression that he was really there to refurbish the flat. He seemed to be engrossed in some kind of work that no one could understand. He had gone down the stairs early, and when he came back to the flat during the day, it was just for a few minutes, as if he had come to collect something he had forgotten in his room.

The parlour in the al-Shibanis' flat was empty as the day approached for Nabil's visit to Switzerland. The letter had come, he said. After that he stood endlessly in front of the mirror, watching himself walk towards it or taking a sidelong look at himself. He marched down the stairs as if they were the steps of a plane.

His movements became more convulsive when he left the door of the flat and went down to the street. He went down slowly, his chest puffed out, jangling his keys, giving an impression of how beautiful his imaginary car was going to be. He was dressed completely in white, his shoes were a shiny black. When he failed to greet Madame Laure, Nabiha al-Shibani told her that he just might not have noticed her, or might have been distracted thinking about the details of his imminent journey.

My aunt was consumed with curiosity and paid little attention to his behaviour. For that reason she did not listen much to Madame Laure when she started commenting on the boy's snobbery and his mother's indifference. My aunt spent the days before Nabil's departure sticking close to the family. It was as if she, too, were waiting for the imaginary fortune to fall out of the sky. Nabiha al-Shibani would ask her a question which she would answer, only for Nabiha al-Shibani to ask her the question again. They repeated the same question and the same answer, as if they shared some secret understanding and excited dream about the good times to come.

Samia was now so used to the school that she barely noticed when the house was suddenly stripped of its furniture. She took no part in the mounting argument about the inheritance. She liked the school, and her mother chose to explain Samia's lack of interest in Nabil's journey as symptomatic of her scepticism about everything Nabil said and did. Samia had stopped speaking to them; she kept up the small habits she had adopted since starting work at the school. She would pass by with her satchel of books and sandwiches. She went out early and came home late.

My aunt thought her persistent absence was due to the quiet relationships she had struck up with several men. She drew this conclusion from an Arab film she had seen at some point in the past. According to the film, plain girls were liable to give in to quick and fleeting relationships. She was absolutely certain that Samia would never marry; in fact, Samia herself was beset by the same feelings. She talked, in front of my aunt, about the young girls who crossed the street or went to the park, as if she herself were a man who admired them. There was, in her words, an indirect acknowledgement that she was a little older and less beautiful than she might wish.

She did not get involved in the travel plans Nabil and his mother were making. When her sister Katya visited, she did not discuss the coming fortune with her. She asked her about other things, about their house, her husband, and whether she was suffering any of the hardships of pregnancy. Katya's legs had grown rounder, and her belly a little higher, and she did not once stop talking, in her loud voice, from the moment she and her husband set foot in the flat.

Nabil departed and sent a telegram on his arrival; this was followed by another after his meeting with the lawyer, and a third telling them that he was coming home and giving a date. He did not stay long in Switzerland, but brought presents when he came back – so many presents of so many different types and sizes, that when his mother opened his suitcases she thought he must have spent his whole time shopping. Most of them were for a woman Nabil would not talk about. He told his sister that she was a divorced woman who had lived with her husband for only a few months. My aunt began to call the fur he had brought this woman by its difficult foreign name. She said that it alone had cost as much as a new car, not to mention the many dresses and expensive perfumes he had also brought home.

On the staircase none of his mannerisms had changed: still

the high head and slow descent from floor to floor. He had his keys in his hand, but this time there really was a car at the entrance. It was big and white with red leather seats. When he started the engine and drove off, the neighbours who saw him were sure that he was going to crash into the wall at the intersection by the park.

My aunt had never imagined that Said al-Shibani's fortune could be that huge. Nabil never went out wearing the same suit twice, and his mother, while changing none of her daily habits, now talked to my aunt and Madame Laure about the incredible furniture she was going to put in the parlour and bedroom. She went back to her old habit of standing in the middle of the room and pointing her finger in all directions.

She changed her mind many times about how best to furnish the parlour. On each occasion, she would stand on the bare tiles between my aunt and Madame Laure and imagine a new way to. arrange the furniture that was coming. She would not buy a new piano. But if Katya wanted a piano, she would send her one at home.

Nabiha al-Shibani had a powerful desire to gather the family together. She was keen to have them all remain close and spent all her time trying to get them to her flat. And so when Nabil brought the divorced woman home, she did not act in the reserved manner my aunt had expected, but took a great interest in her, giving her the feeling that she was not merely a passing guest.

The woman spoke in the dialect of her village, and Nabiha al-Shibani's facial expression relaxed pleasantly when she heard her pronounce certain letters. She did not forget her first marriage, though. As she closed the door behind her son and his lover, she imagined them embracing without any preliminaries, and when she left them in the flat and went up to my aunt's flat, she was sure they would be in bed before she had taken a single step on the stairs.

Samia was happy for the divorced woman. Indeed, she was often alone with her and they had endless conversations. Samia loved to play the role of the bridegroom's loving sister, although she rarely spoke to her brother, and no longer showed the same affection for her mother. She had grown apart from them and her home, and though the upheaval caused by the new situation grew ever noisier around her, she showed little interest in it. It was as if she had become a visitor in her own family.

Part Three

Mathilde would not have listened so closely had it not been for her fear of the footsteps she heard on the stairs, and of the sounds that she imagined came from the other rooms. Recently, as she lay in bed, she had felt unable to prevent the rooms becoming more distant, and more full of strange sounds. They were like locked, empty houses: the kitchen, the big rear balcony, the long hallway from the door, the neighbouring bedroom, the shadows in the corners of the parlour when night fell . . . She could no longer depend on the comfort of her friendship with Madame Khayyat, who now stayed in her flat more and more out of fear that someone might take it over. She had returned not to live in the flat but only to guard it, yet she was always on the verge of leaving. She had packed her bags, locked the bedrooms and draped the furniture in the parlour with large white sheets.

Mathilde wouldn't even have opened her door to him if it had not been for the shells roaring over the house, and crashing into neighbouring buildings. When the bombardment got worse, she left her bedroom, which was vulnerable, and lived in the little hallway between the room with the Western-style bath and the bedrooms. She had prepared for this by putting a chair opposite the solid structural wall and a gas light she could turn on while sitting on the chair. When she had grown used to the shelling, she would go to the chair, not hurrying, not taking her time, but at her usual pace, as if on her way to do some household chore. She would take her seat after making sure that the chair was secure in the corner, and would wake up after a time to find that the shelling had stopped.

Madame Khayyat could not coax Mathilde out of her isolation, nor could the other neighbours. When she was frightened, she would pretend that her world extended no further than the closed door of her flat; that her neighbours' flats were distant, separate houses which had no connection with her. Madame Laure's flat was cut off from above and below, and my aunt's high-up flat was vulnerable to the bombs, as open as a bare roof. On her chair in the narrow hallway, she often thought of the Russian lady hiding in her flat on the ground floor. She thought of her squeezing her small body into a corner of the flat, her face turned to the wall, oblivious of her husband, who would be hidden somewhere else in the flat.

There were now other tenants in the building whom she did not know. The newlyweds squatting in one of the empty flats took an indomitable pride in the spaciousness of its rooms and the view from its balconies. The flat next door to the Russians on the ground floor was occupied by refugees from the South who had sought shelter there one day a few hours after a long bombardment. Mathilde felt embarrassed when she passed their door, which was always open. The man of the family was tall and thin, and did not care if she or the other tenants saw his family exposed like this.

Standing at the door, hesitating over whether to go in or out, he would look back into the flat and speak loudly so that his wife inside could hear him. She would answer him from the far end of the flat; his voice reached her, hollow and reverberant from its passage through the empty rooms.

At first, Mathilde thought they were the ones who had occupied the laundry next door. She had become used to calling the place 'the laundry' because of the round signboard hanging over its door. The laundry had been empty for a long time, so when people came and moved into it they were not really taking it away from anyone. They found it empty and brought their tools and began to fix old cars that protruded out on to the sidewalk. When Mathilde looked out at the street she noticed that the thick black oil which had collected there did not dissolve. It seeped into the pavement, the wall of the park, and the entrance of her own building.

Mathilde thought they had occupied both the flat and the laundry because when she looked over the balcony, she would sometimes see the man from the flat standing at the door of the shop, smoking, or sitting on a little chair. Belatedly she realized that a different lot of refugees had taken over the laundry. They had brought with them not only the family in the flat beside the Russians, but the people who now worked in the makeshift shops that had sprung up all down the street.

During the day, the sound of hammering on the metal bodies of cars could be heard in every corner of the building. Mathilde could not get used to this and began to long for that hour in the late afternoon when the hammering stopped and the shops closed. She would then come out on to the balcony, into the gentle breeze of sundown. She would look down at the gleaming black oil stains before going back inside, her nostrils filled with the fragrance of the fruit of the china bark tree, mingled with the trickling oil, warmed by the heat of the sun.

She did not know why the refugees kept walking up to the other floors of the house. She saw them going up and down the stairs as if they had relatives in the upper flats, or as if they enjoyed looking down on the street from a high place.

The ground-floor flat's new tenants soon became established. My aunt's husband would pass by and greet them, and chat with the man. They brought beds into the house, and in the early part of the summer, they found an old refrigerator. Their flat became a home, imperceptibly, and eventually they began to lock the door. When the wife opened the door and saw someone, she would now greet them warmly and invite them in.

Mathilde would not have stopped to listen to him had it not been for her fear of the night. He was swarthy and slender, and his hair was cropped so short that the white skin of his scalp was visible on both sides of his head and above his neck. When she was about to close the door, he asked her to wait a little – he had something to say. She hesitated. He told her that he wanted to rent a room, self-contained, and near the door.

When he said that the site of the building suited him because it was near the university, Mathilde peered at the thick book in his hand. His speech became calmer, and as he relaxed he began to find the right words. She let him in and had him sit in the parlour. His words grew more precise as his voice grew softer, and while Mathilde pondered what he was saying, her imagination began to work, calculating distances between the different rooms. In her mind she lodged him in a room and closed the door on him, but then reflected on how close it was to the kitchen and her own bedroom.

When she brought him coffee, he was trying to determine the layout of the rooms. She asked him about his family and his home village. He guessed that she had decided upon a room to rent him from the way she kept gesturing in one direction whenever she spoke of the difficulty of dividing up the flat for a man she did not know. Mathilde could detect something in his accent that linked him to the people from the South who had come into the building and the street during the war, but he was educated; the sort of educated person she had not encountered before. There was an adult wisdom and calm in his voice, and something venerable in his facial features that resembled the elderly people of the rural South.

The al-Shibanis had left their flat after Nabil's return from Switzerland a few months before. They had accumulated so many debts that Nabil and his divorced wife flew off to some place his mother would not talk about. The restaurant, the butcher, and the owner of the grocery shop nearby all began to ask for payment at the same time. When two men from the government came to impound the contents of the flat, they found almost nothing in it. Immediately after them came the landlord, who said that he was not going to force them out; he would negotiate with them, especially as they were original occupants of the building.

Nabiha al-Shibani and her daughter did not leave all at once. My aunt thought that they had said their final goodbyes, but they came back the following day. Nabiha al-Shibani said that she had come to take one of the few household things she had left in the flat. They came again two days later, said their goodbyes again, and then came back once more. The other tenants had grown so used to this that Madame Laure would say to my aunt, when she found it hard to remember something, that she would ask Nabiha al-Shibani about it when she saw her tomorrow. They kept dropping by. When Mathilde saw them coming up the stairs she no longer felt that she needed even to greet them.

When they left for good, though, it was really sudden. My aunt and Madame Laure said that Nabiha al-Shibani kept coming back to them because she had nowhere else to live. They left and never came back, and my aunt began to imagine them standing in a street in some distant part of Beirut, looking up at some building still under construction. They were waiting, peering at the building which the construction workers were not making much effort to complete. That is how she imagined them, but she couldn't quite place them in one of the new flats, or conceive of their moving to another building.

Her imagination was of no help to her in this; that is why she left them standing there in the street. When the war started again, she began to suppose that the district where the first bullets were fired was not far from where she had left them standing. Because she had been unable to move them before the war broke out, she began to think that waves of fighting occurred all around them while they stood in their place. The bullets whizzed past, but they could not hear a thing.

Madame Laure, who loved happy endings, said that Nabil had taken them away, to the country to which he had emigrated. She envied them. She said that their flat would remain empty until they came back to it. She couldn't imagine it occupied by anyone else, and when she saw the refugees coming slowly up the stairs and guessed that they had come to squat there, she rushed up to my aunt, trembling, her words muddled and incoherent.

My aunt stopped them from tearing the door down. She even prevented them from going up the few remaining steps that led to the flat. She suddenly seemed strong and capable of violence, and spoke cuttingly in her fiercest southern dialect. They went back down again, and she returned to her flat so calm and confident that no one would have thought she had performed a deed that had stunned Madame Laure and had prompted even Mathilde and Madame Khayyat to visit her in the early evening.

She looked after the al-Shibani flat. When the landlord found out what had happened, he sent her his key so that she could store things there and keep an eye on the place every now and then. She liked the way this made her look in front of the other tenants, so she began to take fastidious care of the flat, visiting it several times a day. Sometimes she even inspected it at night. She would open the door with her key, go in, and stroll through the rooms. She would stand for a while on the big rear balcony. Before returning to her own flat, she would be sure to ring Madame Laure's doorbell to exchange a few brief words with her, after which she would sedately mount the stairs.

She took the greatest care of the al-Shibanis' flat. With the passage of time, she began to talk as if it would be her decision as to whom it would be rented. If she did not like the prospective tenant, she declared, she would not let him past the door.

When Mathilde and Madame Khayyat came to visit her for the second time, she thought she should make an extra effort for appearance's sake. She liked the fact that the tenants were like one big family. If she needed anything, she got it at Madame Laure's or asked Madame Khayyat for it. She suggested that they should enclose the entrance to the building with a big iron gate. They agreed with her and, after an earnest discussion, Madame Laure took a sheet of paper and wrote down the names of all the building's occupants.

Madame Laure put a tick beside the name of those who had agreed to share the cost of the gate. She went to each flat, but something always prevented her from finishing the project. She would start over again, knocking on doors, and on each occasion my aunt could not understand who it was who was making difficulties. Mathilde was enthusiastic about the gate. Even when she resumed her isolation in her flat, she kept asking Madame Laure whenever she saw her whether the neighbours had all agreed yet, and when the gate would be installed.

My aunt and Mathilde quarrelled over the water. My aunt said that she was helping Mathilde by sending her a bucket or two when water was hard to get. She sent her children to fill buckets from the public tap in the park. They went down many times with buckets to fill up the big plastic barrel my aunt had bought at the start of the war. When it was filled, she would send her children on one last trip, this time for Mathilde's water. She was happy to do this. Now, however, as soon as Mathilde heard the sound of water filling the pipes that ran along the bathroom windows, she would rush inside and fill the bathtub and saucepans and every other pot she could find, and this would prevent the water from collecting in the common cistern. My aunt did not, of course, keep silent about this, but Mathilde slammed her door on my aunt and retreated inside, leaving my aunt shouting at the closed door.

Ahmad al-Siblini rented the al-Shibanis' flat. His big over-
hanging belly did not prevent him from being very nimble on
his feet. He signed a lease with the landlord before the other
tenants knew about it. When he brought his wife to the
house, my aunt could not hide her anger. She said she might
just as well have left the flat open for anyone to come and
squat in it.

Yet from the very first, Ahmad al-Siblini's wife seemed
grateful to my aunt for having protected the flat. She talked as
if it had always been her home, even before she had come
here and her husband had signed the lease. She thanked my
aunt effusively. But she criticized Nabiha al-Shibani, whom

she had never met, for her neglect of the appliances and water pipes; Nabiha, she said, had only tended to the outer appearance of the flat.

The builders came after the woman's first visit. They trudged heavily up the stairs, and as soon as they set foot inside the door, the noise began, as if each of them had just gone straight to the worksite assigned him.

When my aunt went down, they had spread out all over the flat. One was ripping out the washstand at the end of the hallway near the Arab-style bathroom, while another swept up the sand from underneath the marble panel that divided the hallway and the entrance to the parlour; a third man had succeeded in removing the two wooden panels from the parlour doorway that led into the other rooms. This is what Ahmad al-Siblini had told the carpenter to do. He did not like the slanting lines cut into the door. They reminded him of scowling faces; he wanted to replace them with new doors made of smooth wood.

They worked on the flat with impressive speed, as if they were racing against the onset of the next battle, which was bound to come after this interval of peace. They paved the big rear balcony with white marble tiles and painted the iron railings. On the two small front balconies facing the park, they very carefully cleaned the rust from the iron. Ahmad al-Siblini lavished special care on the small balconies; and after the workmen were finished with the flat, al-Siblini liked to leave the two doors open so that he could have a clear view of the tops of the tall buildings and the distant horizon of the sea, as he sat on a low chair at the far end of the parlour.

When my aunt saw the view from the open doors, she felt this was a discovery that she ought to have made many years before. She tried the view from different points in the parlour. She sat on the sofa and looked furtively through the inter-laced ironwork of the balcony. She sat in a spot near the corner, looking for some flaw in the scheme of things brought about by opening the doors. But she was finally re-assured by the rhythm of her neighbour's quiet laughter. When she went back to her own flat, however, her enthusiasm for this innovation soon waned and she busied herself with other things.

After Madame Laure saw the open doors, she asked herself why the other tenants had kept the wooden doors closed, blocking that wonderful view for so long. She had not really seen it, somehow, before the new tenants came. She had found nothing unusual in keeping all the doors locked, the wooden doors covered by a glass door and that in turn concealed by a white curtain. Those flimsy white drapes seemed to hang the length of the five floors.

Ahmad al-Siblini's balcony doors were the only ones kept open. The renovations made to the flat made anyone coming up the stairs suppose that the al-Siblinis' balcony had been slightly extended out from the face of the building.

The wife sometimes left her flat in her flowered nightdress and went up to my aunt's flat. She went up the stairs with quick, light steps, pushed the door, which was ajar, fully open, and hurried in. She had started visiting my aunt a couple of days after coming to the house. They sat in the sitting room adjoining the kitchen and chatted. She loved knitting so much that as she hurried down the stairs the movement of her hands on the ball of yarn and knitting needles never stopped.

Ahmad al-Siblini put a white rocker on the big balcony. His wife sat on it and rocked back and forth. Suddenly, with no warning, she would slide off it and race into the kitchen. She moved quickly, so quickly that my aunt thought she was like a little girl. On the stairs, the thin-soled pink slippers came off her feet several times. She would stop, take one step back and slip her foot back inside it, then run to my aunt's flat.

My aunt and Madame Laure still said 'the al-Shibani flat' when they were talking about the al-Siblinis. When I went to visit my aunt, their door on the fourth floor was open, and the light that shone through the balcony doors lit up a rectangle of the hallway near the door. The odour coming out into the hallway was the same as it had always been, and the tiles still glowed with their dark patterns and intertwined flowers. In spite of its obvious cleanliness the flat did not have the shiny gleam of the new, so I thought the old familiar smell must cling to the intricate designs on the tiles.

Mathilde assumed that he would use the flat only to sleep. He would come in early in the evening, greet her, and then go to his room, locking the door. That is what she had imagined when she gave him the spare key and asked him to put off until later any talk of paying rent.

In the two days between her agreement and his coming, she prepared the room that led on to one of the small balconies. It was the best of the three bedrooms, and in order to get to it he had to cross the parlour and the little hallway between the bedrooms and the bathroom. There was no other way. Had she given him the room that opened on to the big balcony, he would have been closer to the kitchen, and she would have felt his presence behind the locked door of the room whenever she went in or out of the kitchen.

When he showed up carrying his cardboard suitcase, Mathilde had the room ready for him. She had taken most of her things out of it, leaving it empty except for the narrow wooden bed and the little table she put in the corner of the room, near the bed.

Mathilde did not sleep the first night he was there. No sooner had she dozed off than she heard his hand grasping the doorknob of the bathroom. When she imagined him squatting over the round bowl, she closed her eyes as though not to hear the jet of his urine streaming against its inner sides. She was now fully awake, but she did not get out of bed despite a powerful wish to do so. She felt that she should not move.

She was on the verge of drifting into a deep sleep when she woke up again. She raised her head suddenly when she heard footsteps in the room where she lay. She peered into the darkness and did not stir, and when the outline of things began to appear before her in the darkness she became certain that there was no one in the room, and that what she had heard had simply been the product of disturbed sleep.

She had not considered the matter of the bathroom when she prepared the room with the small balcony. She had thought he would have satisfied those needs at the university, before coming back to the flat. In the morning she would tell him to use the Arab toilet, even though it was farther for him to get to from his room.

Late in the morning, she was careful to delay going into the bathroom, and when she went in, she spent a long time pouring water into the toilet upon which she then sat, being very careful to let only her thighs rest on the edge of the bowl. He had gone out, leaving the large, spacious flat to her, though she still felt uneasy and anxious when she pushed open the door to his room. There was nothing unusual, it was just as if he had not even slept a whole night in there.

Mathilde was able to guess that he had left early out of embarrassment, and she also guessed that if she were to stand on the small balcony and look out at the park she would see him sitting on one of the chairs scattered around it, waiting for the time of his university class.

She did not actually enter his room; she was even careful not to let her foot touch the marble sill between the hallway and the entrance. She closed the door and walked through the rooms to the kitchen. She could not settle to anything, and when she sat on the sofa in the parlour she felt a desire to go back to bed. But still she couldn't sleep, and only lay stretched out on her back, her feet pressed together.

It was a long day. She had spent the two previous days doing whatever cleaning she could, in anticipation of his coming. She did not know why, nor did she know why she had overdone it – her broom and cloth reaching corners and crannies that no one ever saw.

She got off the bed to have another look at some of the places she had cleaned. She went into the kitchen and opened the little cupboard doors under the sink. She closed the little doors after looking at the floor of the closet and examining the bottles and tins. She peeked on top of the refrigerator and into the corner of the kitchen behind the door. After a while, she went out on to the big balcony and looked down at the watchman's house. Two small children were playing, at some distance from one another. They were so quiet she thought they were not playing the same game. Their mother came out into the sunlight, holding a green plastic basket filled with damp laundry. She did not speak to the children or turn in their direction, but went straight to the empty pool and began to drape the laundry over its sides.

The sun shone hot and bright on the eastern corner of the Russians' balcony. Its cement surface looked incandescent under the blazing light. Mathilde went into her room, lay on her back, pressed her legs together and tried to make herself sleep, shutting the tender fleshy swelling of her eyelids over her blue eyes.

She did not sleep long. The sun reached the edge of the bed, then her legs, and she rose irritably from her nap. She slipped her feet into her worn slippers and went to the refrigerator. Drinking cold water, she suddenly thought she would visit the Russian lady.

By the time she closed the refrigerator door, she had changed her mind, deciding instead to go back to bed. She hurried, her feet stumbling along the tiles. When she was back in bed, she began to calculate how much of the day remained – as if she were waiting for him to come in the early evening.

My aunt paid no attention to the young man who had moved into Mathilde's flat. She got on to that subject only briefly in conversation with Madame Laure. They found little about him to discuss, as if the passing of half a day after his moving into the flat had been ample time in which to deal with him. Since the war had started again, my aunt had been less interested in what went on in the building. She reckoned that the building was living out its last days, and that what it was experiencing now was the chaos that came before the final departure of all the occupants.

She was less interested also in what went on inside the different flats. She let Madame Laure and her husband deal with their own problems behind closed doors. Madame Laure had been thinking about America since the first of the new gun-battles. She dreamed of the deliciously wide streets there, and the fast white or red cars; and when the shelling grew more violent or the fighting intensified, the cars grew even shinier and the streets wider.

My aunt firmly believed that Madame Laure would leave soon. She would have no difficulty living in America, my aunt would say, because she knew how to deal with banks, and Armenians knew how to finesse their letters to their women friends and relatives scattered in so many countries.

But during the ceasefires Madame Laure forgot about travelling and thought no more about it. She forgot the wide streets and the long shiny cars. When a truce lasted for a while, she even made some small repairs to her flat and spoke of the war as if it belonged to the remote past.

On the days after the battles, she could be seen on the steps with her husband. They went on outings or visits. Sometimes he went down the street ahead of her to brush the dust from his old grey car and wipe off the steering wheel and dash-board with a yellow cloth, and then he waited for her to come down.

Abraham, her husband, was now more willing to speak than he had ever been before. He talked and laughed with my aunt's husband at the door of the building, and when he went up the stairs to his flat on the fourth floor he trotted along as though he were a much younger man than he actually was. He had even changed the way he dressed. He no longer always wore suits, or came down the stairs with his calm and confi-dent air. My aunt's husband said he reminded him of a boy on vacation, and he said as well that he had so quickly grown accustomed to the war because Armenians had been used to such things ever since being expelled from Turkey.

In the brisk way he walked up the stairs, he seemed like a man playing the part of a youth, and on one occasion my aunt's husband noticed him puff out his chest and lift his head high as he spoke.

Behind his locked door, he talked to his wife about his shop, which was in the souk. He told her about the sums being offered to him for it – they were all paltry offers, not even amounting to half its original value.

Sometimes he met with other traders from the street where his shop was located. Upon returning he would tell his wife how he would have to wait until things became clearer. When the battles grew fiercer, and there were reports of shops being burned, he rushed downstairs, without giving himself time to check on whether the fighting had started up again, and made his way to the souk. He returned with two suitcases bulging with watches, small alarm clocks, and carriage clocks for tables or shelves.

My aunt guessed that he would not have taken this risk had he not spent his last pound. He put the watches and alarm clocks in the closet after taking them out of the suit-cases and slept well that night. In the morning, his wife went up to my aunt's and asked her, in a slightly subdued tone, to tell her relatives that Abraham was selling his clocks at reduced prices.

My aunt's husband bought a watch with a gold chain, and my aunt told our relatives in the al-Munla district to come and help Madame Laure. Abraham sold two watches to Armenians living in a nearby building. Within a week he had set aside a corner of his flat for repairing watches. There was a chair and a small table with delicate metal tools and his black eyeglass.

My aunt's husband did not believe they needed money that badly. He kept repeating his own theory about Armenians, that they never spent their savings, even when they were about to starve to death. He said that Abraham had locked up his money behind a closet door that he would never open again.

Abraham's shop was burned out a few days after he brought the watches and alarm clocks home. Other shops were burned down in the same street, and in streets nearby. After that he had more and more meetings with the owners of the wrecked shops. They got together and talked about their rights, and once my aunt's husband saw his picture in the newspaper with the other traders. He showed it to my aunt, who ran to Madame Laure clutching the newspaper in her outstretched arms.

Mathilde was waiting for the water to boil in the big pot when she heard a light knocking on the wooden frame of the kitchen door. He was hesitant and confused, and when she looked at him she too hesitated a moment before letting him in. He was carrying a round tray with a teapot on it, obviously a cheap one, but new and shiny. Mathilde stayed where she was while he washed it in the sink, and as he filled it with water she began to think he was stealing quick glances at the lower part of her plump white legs. She momentarily considered turning round or going over to the refrigerator to get away from his furtive glances. She turned her back to the sink, and when she was a few steps away he asked her if she would allow him to put his teapot on the gas.

He had changed from his first day in the flat. Two days before, he had come out of the Western-style bathroom, clean, his hair damp, his slender body lost in his loose grey pyjamas, whose sleeves he had rolled up while wiping from his slippers the water that had dripped from him. He had changed. She should have known that from the beginning, from the time she saw his books stacked up on the table and the bed neatly made up. At sundown he went out and sat on the little balcony. Madame Laure saw him. He was sitting on a chair, enveloped by his pyjamas. Mathilde did not like it, and the following afternoon went out on to the other small balcony to see if he was there once again. She surprised him. He lowered his head and smiled slightly. When she remained standing there, he grew more embarrassed and began to stare fixedly at a point on the top of the china bark trees.

He liked lingering around the flat. His pyjamas and plastic sandals made Mathilde think that in a few days he would start spending all his time there, going back and forth between his room, the balcony, and the bath. He put his wet towel on the arm of the chair to expose it to the air blowing through the door. He was much cleaner than she first thought, and when she looked around his room shortly after he had left, she found everything in its place. The books were on the table, the plastic sandals on the floor by the bed, and the towel on the arm of the chair.

Whenever he left, she had a sudden urge to move about. She wandered among the rooms but found nothing to do. She finished preparing her lunch, and it was still morning. She reclined on her bed or slept, or contemplated a visit to the Russian lady on the ground floor.

When he came home he would ring the doorbell lightly, wait a little, then open the door using his key, as if by ringing the bell he was giving her the time she needed to get away from the hallway between the door and the Arab-style bathroom down at the end. He would enter, and after one step turn right, into the parlour. He would keep his eyes fixed, wary of alighting on anything in the hall. He would go into his room and sit down on the edge of the bed. While removing his shoes, he would listen. He would remove his socks slowly, waiting for the sound of her large white feet moving through the rooms to her bedroom near the kitchen.

He was able to hear her steps moving through the rooms, the kitchen, and on to the big balcony. He would imagine each time that she was taking the lids off pots and looking into their empty interiors. In her room, she would be tucking in the edges of the sheets with light movements, then lying down on the bed.

They were each moving around in their own narrow spaces. Mathilde kept to the kitchen, her bedroom and the balcony between them, and he went no farther than the bathroom. The middle of the flat was an empty space between them, and neither dared cross it. Mathilde did not realize that she was careful not to go near the door to the parlour, or that, when she slept, she lay on the southern part of the bed, leaving empty the side of the bed that was closest to his room.

She awoke abruptly when she heard the thunder of the shell. It exploded so close that Mathilde thought it had landed right beside the building. She kept herself a moment longer in her bed, then went into the bathroom, and came out again just a few moments later, running, propelled by the tremendous impact of the second explosion.

The shock waves made Mathilde misjudge the distance between her foot and the tiles. She nearly fell several times, and when she supported her arm against the wall she felt it shaking, as if a silent missile were exploding inside it. The shelling was very close by now, much closer than usual, and when she went through the parlour door into the small hallway between the Western-style bathroom and the bedrooms, she saw him standing at the doorway to his room. His face was pale, and when he saw her he waited for her to lead him to the corner she used when there was shelling going on.

She sat on the chair in the corner and thrust it against the wall with a sudden movement of her back and feet. He crouched in the other corner, near the door to his room. He was confused and afraid, and looked at her only once, out of the corner of his eye. She told him to move closer to her, and he crept towards the corner near her own. They were much closer to one another, so close that she drew her foot back to leave him more space.

His chest was pressed against his knees, and his arms were locked around his shins. When he glanced in her direction and saw her in her nightdress, his eyes were confused and wet. She was looking down at him from above; he contracted his body and crouched in against himself. When some time had passed after the last missile, he altered his position a little and uttered a few words that Mathilde knew were meaningless. She knew that the shelling had stopped, but did not rise from her chair. He lifted his head in her direction, and when their eyes met he gave a brief, hesitant smile.

No one had ever thought the Russian lady would behave so calmly. She just went into the kitchen, opened the green door that looked out on the new tenants, and motioned for one of the children to come in. It was as if she had even practised it a few times. Every so often she opened the bolt on the door and then closed it, as if to test how quickly she could do it. As to the children out on the vacant lot, it would not have occurred to her to speak to them unless her husband prompted her to. He was the one who had made them friendly and obedient. At first he had stood behind the window and called the nearest of them to come to him.

He called him in a soft voice, but the boy hesitated to come. When the boy moved and took his first step in the man's direction, his brothers had stood motionless, far back on the waste ground.

After that, all the Russian man had had to do was raise his voice, which was always on the verge of a cough, until the nearest boy came over to him. He would make some effort to keep smiling the whole time, while the boy came and went. The boy would go to the store in the high street, and when he came back would find the man waiting on a kitchen chair. Getting up to take the groceries and change from the boy, the man would murmur a few indistinct words to express thanks.

The Russian lady had behaved quite calmly when she learned from the doctor that her husband was living through his last days. He would only hold on for a little longer. When she returned from the doctor there had been no fear or anxiety in her face. She had covered him up, up to his chin. She had asked him whether he was hungry, and had sat down on a chair near him, beside the bed.

She even remained calm when she motioned for the boy to approach. She told him to tell Mathilde that her husband was dead. The boy went up to the third floor, and a few moments later the Russian lady heard Mathilde hurrying urgently down the stairs, and knew that she did not care about the loud noise her feet were making.

Mathilde came into the flat, and the first thing she thought of was finding a way to make the Russian lady open the doors and windows, to dispel the odour that gave the impression that the flat had been closed on its occupants for years. He was laid out on the bed, his silver-framed eye-glasses lay on the end-table. Mathilde looked at the locks of brown hair tousled on his forehead and ears. She said to herself that his hair had not changed much. His features were still attractive, suggesting the kind of life he had lived when he came here as a young man. Mathilde imagined him nimble and active, moving from his front door to the iron railing of his balcony and the high entrance to the building. A lock of his smooth hair lay on his face no matter how she turned or brushed it away.

The three of them spent a considerable time in the flat. Mathilde was unable to do anything but ask the Russian lady the same questions over and over again. It was as if he were asleep in the next room, with the door open. She stole a glance at him every now and then. The woman's answers made her certain that they needed someone to help them, otherwise the man would stay laid out this way for ever.

By the time Abraham the Armenian came down, the heads of the new tenants' children were silently lined up in a row along the balcony railing, as if they were waiting for a sight or sound that would start them talking. Abraham went into the flat. Mathilde told him she did not know what to do. She turned to him, standing at a distance from the Russian lady, and told him that the woman did not know the address of a single person, only her daughter's telephone number in London.

The poor man living in the watchman's house stayed standing at the door; he would not come inside. When Abraham invited him to come in, he said that he had only come to ask whether there was anything he could do. The Russian lady had not told Abraham anything useful. When he asked her about the woman that she used to visit in the al-Munla district, she only murmured a few indistinct words. Then she repeated that she knew her daughter's telephone number. When he pressed her to remember whether they knew anyone in Beirut, she left him and went to look through her husband's things in the closet.

She searched for a long time before finding a folded sheet of paper in the pocket of a suit on a hanger. While he could read the number, he could not make out the name of the person whose number it was. The woman said that this was 'the committee's' number, and he told her that she should be the one to talk to them. She waited a long time on the telephone until someone answered. When she spoke, it was in a few brief, calm words, from which Abraham understood only that she remembered how to speak Russian.

Mathilde had opened two of the windows that looked out on to the wall of the neighbouring building by the time Umm Ibrahim al-Kilani came into the flat. As usual, she was nervous and did not know what to say or whom to greet, and sat down in a corner.

When the man from the watchman's house came for the second time, he stayed at the door. He rang the doorbell after realizing that no one inside would hear his light knock. He had a little coffee pot and some cups which Abraham took from him, and once back inside, he served the coffee himself to the silent women. There were a few extra cups on the tray, and Abraham poured one for himself. When his wife and my aunt came in, he laid his hand on the pot to test its heat.

When Madame Laure suggested that they open more windows, her husband looked muddled and asked Mathilde which window he should open. Mathilde did not answer, but looked directly at him as if she was considering his question. Umm Ibrahim al-Kilani told him from her corner to open the windows in the kitchen and the room next door to it. This was the first time she had spoken since her arrival, and even though she had only said a few words, they were sufficient to help her relax in her chair for the next few minutes. She would have liked to speak again, but Mathilde's silent face did not encourage her to do so.

When the two men came in, an old car waited for them with its driver in front of the entrance to the building. Abraham greeted them. One of them was short and warmly dressed despite the mild weather. He spoke broken Arabic with Abraham, and he and his colleague went into the room where the Russian man was laid out on the bed. They were old men, and Abraham guessed that they were old friends of the Russian. When the Russian lady saw them coming towards her, her body began to shake and she started to cry like a little girl. She spoke to them in tearful Russian while backing up a couple of steps, until she bumped into a chair. She sat down on it and began to cry softly.

They were so old that Abraham supposed they must be the last remaining members of 'the committee'. Madame Laure got up and made them coffee which they did not drink, but they were polite, and despite their slow movements they seemed to know exactly what to do.

It was as if the dead Russian came from a quite different country from theirs. Even laid out on his bed, an air of nobility had not left his face. He looked like the son of an old feudal lord. When Mathilde reminisced about the early days of the building, she still pictured him as a young man, coming out of the door of his flat as if he were descending the gangway of an ocean liner.

One of the old men stood at the door of the flat and motioned to the driver leaning against the door of the car. The driver came closer and gave the old man a pen and sheet of paper, which he took back from him a few moments later. He hurried to the car, started it and sped off.

The man went back inside and turned to the Russian lady and my aunt supposed that they were talking about the cost of burial. The Russian lady shook her head as if refusing something being offered to her. It appeared that he was insisting, from the way she continued to shake her head and the way her voice took on a plaintive tone, as if she were about to start crying again. The man retreated a little, and seemed about to go and sit with the other guests.

The two old men did not delay in taking charge of things in the flat. Abraham found himself sitting on the sofa waiting for the little Russian man to give him something to do. The other old man kept a distance from his colleague. He walked around the spacious room, but distractedly. He seemed older than his compatriot, but moved more quickly. Mathilde ignored the short man when he came towards her. My aunt said that he must have taken Mathilde for a Russian like himself.

When the driver came back, he got out quickly from his car and looked back at the procession stretching out behind him. It was a whole motorcade. There was a grey hearse and two cars behind, each decorated with a large floral wreath. When the cars stopped, two priests got out of one of them, and went directly to the room where the Russian was laid out. After several minutes, they re-emerged. They all moved so quickly that the Russian lady could scarcely believe that her husband was already inside the grey hearse. The two old men wasted no time, nor did the priests; they were carrying out the traditional rituals, to the letter. But they gave her no time to linger over him as he was carried out of the house, and the tenants had no chance to gather around and grieve with her, or to show her affection for the first time in the many years they had lived in the building.

Umm Ibrahim al-Kilani would repeatedly tell the refugees on the ground floor that the Russian lady was lonely, and that she could die with no one even knowing. She urged the wife to knock at her door every now and then. Lately, Umm Ibrahim al-Kilani had been having even stronger premonitions of the Russian lady's imminent death. She had begun to lean over the railing at the far end of her big balcony and look down at the Russian's closed kitchen window, in the hope of seeing a shadow or movement inside the dim kitchen.

The refugee's wife refrained from pressing the doorbell because she thought of the distance the Russian lady would have to walk in order to answer the door. She would always stop herself at the last moment, and limit herself to asking the children about her. She called loudly from the door of her kitchen and when one of the children came to her she would ask him – still very loudly – when he had last seen the Russian lady.

Mathilde visited her after her husband's death, but infrequently. She sat beside her on the sofa and asked her household questions, about her food and laundry. The Russian woman's answers were brief, and then she resumed her silence. Mathilde began to visit even less frequently, and felt, whenever she started down the stairs, that she ought to prepare herself, as if she were making a visit to some remote place.

The wife of the man living in the watchman's house told her children that if the Russian lady were to stick her head out of the door, they were to be sure to ask her if she had any dirty laundry. This woman pitied the Russian lady so much that she told her husband to persuade the children to carry a dish of food to her every day. Her feelings were genuine, and whenever she carried out her plastic basket filled with damp laundry, she would slow down in front of the Russian lady's window, as if willing her to give her some dirty clothes.

When the Russian lady called to one of her children, the refugee's wife, who was a huge woman, hurried to the window and unleashed a stream of words at the old woman, and understood when it was over only that she had not been understood. The Russian lady stared at her rather coldly, and when the woman said nothing more, continued to look at her for a few moments, her face not betraying the slightest movement. Suddenly, as they were staring at one another, the huge woman began a new round of brief but animated explanations, and this time she gesticulated with her hands too, grasping her dress by the neck and pulling it up a little, and balling up her fingers and pretending to feed herself.

Umm Ibrahim al-Kilani never saw the Russian lady's laundry on the clothes line in the corner of her big balcony. Sometimes she leaned over the railing, almost falling off in her attempts to see the place where the woman hung her laundry. Clearly she had not washed any of her clothes for a long time: the wooden clothes pegs never moved from their place on the line. A woman of her age did not dirty her clothes much, Umm Ibrahim reasoned. She did not sweat, for example, since her kitchen window prevented the sun reaching even as far as the edge of the sink.

The child ran, a banknote in his hand, towards the iron gate that opened on to the street, and when he reached it he waited a little so that one of his brothers could catch up with him. When they returned, they found the old lady waiting for them, sitting on the very same chair on which her husband would sit when he used to wait for them. The boy offered the groceries in both hands. The Russian lady ate only tinned food, the refugee woman told her husband as they sat, with their children, around their big platter of food. When the man looked interested, one of the children said that she cooked sardines from the tin, and the smell that came out of her kitchen window was like burning oil.

When the Russian lady died, Mathilde guessed that several days had passed before any of the occupants of the building knew a thing about it. The shelling had been extremely fierce in recent days, so much so that all those in the exposed watchman's house were forced to get out for a while. The refugees on the ground floor, in the flat next door to the Russian lady's, knew she was dead from the smell that eventually came out of the two small windows of the Arab-style bathroom. They did nothing themselves when they became certain that there was no one alive inside. They did not remove the door, nor did the man climb from his balcony through one of the open windows. Instead, the woman went up to Mathilde's flat. Mathilde came downstairs immediately, as boldly as if she knew exactly what to do. But when she reached the door, she stopped. She stood there baffled, and waited for the refugee to tell her what to do next.

When he opened the door from the inside, he had his hand pressed over his nose and mouth. He went out quickly to the entrance hall of the building. Mathilde did not go in, but waited for someone else to go in before her and open the windows which the Russian lady had kept firmly closed for so long.

Once inside, she knew why the woman had not hung her laundry on the line in the corner of the balcony. She knew from the heap of clothes the woman had piled up in her bedroom, on the floor between the bed and the closet. It was a confused and enormous pile, on to which the Russian lady had put the entire contents of the closets, and had been lying there for a long time. The heap contained some of her husband's clothes, as well. She had resorted to this after all her clothes were dirty, and there was nothing left in her closet.

The kitchen was littered with empty tins. Mathilde saw how the woman had not even put herself to the trouble of collecting the empty tins in one place. Mathilde did not stay long inside the flat. She hurried up to her own flat, as if to talk things over with him, but he was not at home. She went to

Madame Laure, who in turn went up to see my aunt, and my aunt wasted no time – she was even faster than Madame Laure had expected. She went down to the clinic in the building next door and told the people she saw there that the woman had been dead for days.

The ambulance took away only the woman's body, leaving the flat just as it was. The refugee sealed it up by positioning a wooden plank across the double doors and nailing it in place. As his powerful hammer-blows fell on the plank and the nails, Mathilde, my aunt, and Madame Laure stood beside him in silence, as if supervising a process that required observers and witnesses.

Mathilde went back up to her flat. She opened the door with the key that was still warm in her fist, and tottered inside. She had rearranged the rooms; she now slept in the room next to his. Only the little hallway and the Western-style bathroom separated the rooms where they slept. And she had put new furniture in his room. She had taken the clothes rack and put it in the corner behind the door, and given him two more chairs for guests that might come to visit him from the university.

He would put on his pyjamas as soon as he arrived home, and recently had begun to stroll freely through the rooms. He went into the kitchen at dinnertime, and sat at the table across from Mathilde. Many things had changed between them. She told Madame Laure that he gave her extra money for the food she served him twice a day, but the maid on the fourth floor of the next building once saw him going into her room and coming out of it while she was lying on the bed. The wooden shutter was open, and when Mathilde saw the maid looking into the room, she got up and closed the shutter, and slammed the window shut.

From the time he had started going into her room, he had been more active and assertive around the flat. He now opened the cabinets and peered into the closets and corners and at the furniture in the salon. He could not get enough of exploring the flat. Mathilde still lay in her bed while he moved from room to room. She imagined his movements and the position of his hands on the shelves of the closet or on top of the refrigerator. When he spoke to her before returning to his room to sleep, he looked down coolly at her neck and at her feet pressed firmly together on her bed.

When he came home to the flat that evening, he found that Mathilde had taken all the folded clothes out of the closets and was refolding them. She was confused and worried. When he entered her room, she greeted him listlessly and continued folding the clothes and putting them back on the closet shelves. He asked her about the wooden plank across the door of the Russian lady's flat. She replied without lifting her head. His eyes narrowed, and suddenly his thin face looked like that of an old man from the South.

Although he visited her bedroom and roamed freely through the many rooms of the flat, she was often taken aback by his sudden presence behind her in the kitchen or one of the other rooms. She suddenly sensed him, as if he had not come through the door, or as if he had already been there before she entered. She would be shaken for a few moments, then speak only in order to say something and hear his reply. When she went out before he did, her back shrank from him, as if wary of a hand touching her or pushing her forward.

She told him nothing more about the Russian lady and at

dinnertime she asked him to go into the kitchen alone. She remained seated before the closet door. When he had finished eating, he went to his room through the long hallway and parlour. He avoided looking at her again. He locked the door of his room and opened it only to go to the bathroom.

Madame Laure found the repairs she had made to her flat sufficient once she had had the outer door and the wall around it painted yellow. The entrance to her flat now stood out from the stairway wall, and made the entrance to the other flats seem antiquated. On the lower floors, the children's hands had dug long lines into the stairway walls. A child would hold a metal blade against the wall and then walk down a flight or two of stairs, and in some spots a light punch from the fist of a mischievous boy was enough to knock off a large round layer of paint. Many successive layers and colours of paint had fallen off; Madame Laure was surprised by just how many times the stairway had been painted before she had come to the building.

She gave the impression she was still making improvements to her flat because she did not want the neighbours accusing her of laziness. She was afraid she would lose her desire to do housework, especially as on many days she failed to do more than wipe down the two glass panes in the door. She had begun to feel the uselessness of the work, and when she looked at the three-storey brick building next door, with the Popular Clinic occupying its ground floor, she knew that people who looked at the two buildings from a distance would realize how vain and wasted the effort expended had been. The wooden shutters of the brick building next door were broken and hung open. The gaps caused by a few bricks falling from the roof suggested that no one lived on the top two floors. The woman next door who used to stand looking out of her window, leaning her head on the white sill, had long gone. The only movement in the building was that of the clinic staff on the ground floor.

Madame Laure, who had been the first to tile her balcony, knew very well that weakness and exhaustion was seeping into the building. She looked from one balcony to another, and saw dust and dirt collected along the sides and in the corners. She said that the residents had begun to retreat into the building, towards the inner rooms. In the sunny daytimes they looked out from the small balconies that overlooked the park and locked the doors when they came back inside.

She still dreamed of America, but the cars there had resumed their ordinary size. When she daydreamed now, she no longer found herself standing by a wide street with flowers, lawns and plants of uniform height. Influenced by

American television programmes, she had begun to say that America was like any other country – in the neighbourhoods where black people lived, she said, you saw ugliness no better than the overcrowded neighbourhoods of Beirut.

She no longer thought of travelling. When her husband began to think the subject over, she tried to find a way of diverting him from his dreams. He now looked different when he came into the flat. The light and cheerful air he adopted on the stairs was deflated. He no longer came in with his head high and his sleeves rolled halfway up his arms. Weariness came over him as soon as she opened the door for him; he stepped inside and drew a long breath, which ended with his chest sagging and his shoulders hunched. He went directly into the sitting room. When he looked at the chair and table she had set up for him to repair the watches, he asked her why she had left them there. His inclination to fix the watches had been short-lived, and vanished completely a few days after she had prepared the chair and table. He asked his wife to stop telling people that he was working at home, and insisted on this. When my aunt came to him with a broken watch belonging to one of our relatives, he did not look happy. My aunt told her relatives that he had fixed it begrudgingly.

During the moments when the shelling intensified, all he had was his wife, whom he resented because she kept him from travelling. The shells fell near and around the building, but he would merely wait for the shelling to stop and for morning to come so that he could go directly to the American Embassy. Then, by morning, he would have forgotten the idea. And yet as he walked through the flat, he felt pangs of impatience; he raised his voice and shouted angry words in Armenian. My aunt could hear them in her flat upstairs. It was always just one long sentence, which he pronounced in his loud, resonant voice before falling silent. My aunt knew that Madame Laure trembled before him and that she put her hand over her mouth to urge him to silence.

The flat depressed him but he lingered in it all day. My aunt told Madame Laure that homes were not made for men. She said that she had said all kinds of nice things to encourage him to go out, but it was no use. The businessmen were no longer meeting to discuss their demands. When she asked him about it now, all he said was that the whole matter had become politicized.

My aunt said that Abraham was good-hearted and she compared him to her husband, who never spent two consecutive hours in the flat. On the occasions when the shelling upset him my aunt's husband became unbearable. He interfered in everything, big and small, and asked questions which provoked replies designed to allow him to pick a fight.

Later on, Abraham had no objection to working in the bakery my aunt's husband had bought. At first my aunt did not believe it, but when she saw him dusted with white patches of flour, she was sure that he was not just delivering bread by truck to restaurants; that he really did work with the scaffolds of baked bread and the dough machines. He moved quickly through the bakery, and chatted with everybody, showing that no work was beneath him.

My aunt saw him on the stairs, now contented and enthusiastic. She recalled what her husband had said about his enjoyment of the work, and he fell in her estimation. When she saw him, his trousers blotchy with flour, she couldn't help noticing more than before his prominent bony feet, and how his wide shoes flapped, loose and worn at the front.

Madame Laure began to spend more time at my aunt's once her husband started working at the bakery. Nothing about her had changed, in my aunt's view; only Abraham had changed. When her husband told her that Abraham talked too much and had a hard time with the customers, this confirmed to her how insufferable he must really be.

My aunt's son was sleeping in Madame Khayyat's flat when the explosion sounded. His wife shook him awake, thinking that the bomb had landed on the roof of the building. He awoke immediately, and when he saw shattered glass on the bed, and on him, he ran to where his son of a few months old was sleeping. He did not think about his wife; he did not speak to her. When his son was in his arms, he leaped to the door, but when he opened it, he could not see the staircase, only a few steps hanging against the wall; the treads were broken up and splintered here and there. He was able to slow down and stop himself; otherwise he and his son would have fallen all the way to the ground floor of the building. He retreated back inside, his son still crying in his arms.

Madame Khayyat had lent him her flat after swearing on oath to herself that she would not come back until the war was over. She had given him the use of everything in the apartment and had not closed off even one of the rooms. His slender, dark-skinned wife would wander through the large rooms in the spacious flat, then, every little while, she would go into the room where her husband slept, sprawled out on the mattress. She knelt by him and contemplated him sleeping, her elbow resting on the limp rubber cushion.

Madame Khayyat had left after taking some of her belongings – more than she had ever taken before. She was frightened by what had happened to Mathilde. In the few days she had spent in the flat afterwards, she did not even dare to go into the bathroom beside her room. She even became afraid of the little balcony and the stairs.

My aunt had speedily consented to the idea of her son and his wife living in Madame Khayyat's flat on the third floor; it was safer than her exposed flat. He and his wife moved downstairs to this flat with its old and heavy furniture, and as soon as he had crossed the threshold her son had begun to think up ways of staying on there even after the war was over.

It was now as if my aunt owned two flats in the building. When one of her female relatives rang the bell from the entrance she would look down from the top of the stairwell on the fifth floor, and instruct her to come up to the third floor – there she would receive her guests. My aunt would get to the flat first, and once there, would act with exaggerated familiarity.

The man on the second storey fell all the way down when he opened his door to walk towards his living room, where he wanted to hide. He fell on to the heaps of debris. When he regained consciousness, he looked up and saw how stones and entire slabs of plaster had fallen from his flat.

His flat and the al-Kilani flat were the most heavily damaged flats in the building. He was alone there. He had sent his family up to the mountain, far from the shelling, and stayed behind to take care of what was left of his business.

The next day, the passers-by who stopped to look stared for a long time at the second floor. All that was left of it were empty shattered rooms, open to the pedestrians' view. A towel still hung from the metal ring near the washstand, and some of the pots and pans in the kitchen had fallen out of the open cabinets and were scattered in what was left of the hallway, and on the rubble that covered the ground floor. The pedestrians could see the rest of the flat as if they had sneaked in to peek furtively around at the sofa in the corner, the lamp, and the wallpaper. The hanging towel suggested a woman had just left the room and was still walking down the hallway.

The staring pedestrians were not impressed by the al-Kilani flat. The exposed inside wall was stained with dirty handprints, and marked with childish words and phrases scrawled in crayon. Pictures of round faces with long lines extending from their crowns, like rays of the sun, were drawn towards the bottom of the same wall. The al-Kilani flat appeared to be bare, from what one could see of it. Umm

Ibrahim had not hung anything on the wall, or hung a towel on a ring. The refugee's flat on the ground floor was also empty. He and his wife had carried out their few possessions and taken them back to their village.

Few of the tenants were there when the missile exploded. The women had left in terror after what happened to Mathilde. Some of them were even afraid when they were out on the stairwell, so they moved as quickly as they could while going up or down. What frightened my aunt most was the Arab-style bathroom in Mathilde's flat. She saw that the flood of water that had run on to the tiles had not been enough to wash away the rancid remains of the dried blood. She was terrified by the thought of what happened there, and her fear extended to her own bathroom – whenever she walked past the door or groped for the light switch on the wall just inside it, she trembled and the hairs rose on her neck. She felt a sudden weakness in her stomach when she imagined Mathilde lying on the tiles, the veined and emaciated hands moving over her body.

There were few tenants left. The family in the watchman's house had fled because of the unusually violent shelling in the days before the building was hit. The zinc roof of their house had nearly fallen in from the continuous reverberations. The noise alone had been enough to make the house lean over to one side. The man had urged his wife and children to hurry, as if a missile had an imminent appointment to fall in the middle of this patch of ground. The driver of the car that was waiting for them in front of the building was even more insistent. He threatened them, saying that he would throw away their bundles of clothing and the luggage they had locked in the boot of the car and lashed to its roof.

The passers-by who crowded in front of the building after the explosion said that someone had planted a bomb inside. My aunt, in her description of what had happened to the building, said that it was like a hollowed-out aubergine. She stood underneath the stairs and looked up. She said that the landlord had removed the stairs from the building so that the occupants would no longer be able to go up or down.

Madame Laure had heard nothing unusual in Mathilde's flat that night. When she stood on the stairs among her neighbours, while the police were leading him outside, she was shaking and hid behind my aunt. She told the investigators that she knew nothing about the incident. He had come to Mathilde's flat and slept and eaten there for a monthly rent. She told them that she did not even know which room he slept in.

She was afraid of him on the stairs, though he was surrounded by their rifles and khaki uniforms, and the other neighbours were afraid of him too. When my aunt spat at him in front of the policemen, none of them stopped her. She shouted words at him that sounded to the officers like the phrases used in television courtrooms. Only my aunt avenged Mathilde by spitting at him. Though she missed, the effect was as though she had given him a powerful slap on the face. Madame Khayyat was so frightened that she could not even look at him.

No one in the building was able to sleep that night. Madame Laure kept imagining that she could smell the stench coming from the window of Mathilde's Arab bathroom. She asked her husband what they would do with Mathilde's flat. When the investigators and policemen left, she saw for the first time a red wax seal. It was real wax, only red. When she passed the door, going up or downstairs, her steps were brisker and she did not feel safe until she had reached the next landing.

The locked door did not reassure her. She still imagined ghosts, voices, and blood staining the tiles in wide tracks. She also reckoned that the locks did not prevent fear but increased it. She imagined the ghosts moving, changing the look of the flat and the placement of the furniture. When she sat on her bed before going to sleep, for the first time she began to think about what was happening directly below her in Mathilde's flat.

She and her husband were sleeping in their separate beds when the bomb exploded. Abraham was the only one in the building who headed for the big balcony. He saw nothing there. He assumed that once again he had been mistaken about where a shell had fallen. His wife called to him from the door, and when he brought his head closer, peering down, he saw a dense dust-cloud that blocked his view of the ground-floor entrance. He shouted down, but no one replied, though a few moments later he heard the second-floor man land on the pile of masonry and plaster.

Abraham wanted to help but there was nothing he could do. The stairs to the lower floors had collapsed or been smashed, and when he tried to go up, to the fifth floor, his wife prevented him, afraid of more collapses. The al-Siblini flat near him was still locked despite the fact that two panes of glass had fallen from their frames in the door. His wife grabbed him and pulled him inside. They stood in the kitchen, looking from the doorway out at the big balcony. A cool breeze blew. He told his wife to shut off the butane-gas canister.

The explosion had come two full hours after the shelling had stopped. When he heard voices in the street, he knew that men from the al-Munla district had come to see what had happened to the building.

People gathered around the two police cars, and some of them even went into the building and stood at the steps on the ground floor. My aunt said that they would not do anything to the young man. When he came through the door, his hands shackled, he was talking incessantly. He was speaking with self-conscious clarity. When my aunt cursed him, it was as if she were answering him in the same lawyerly language. He did not stop speaking, and when he turned to look in her direction, she became afraid and retreated a few steps. But she returned to the charge and one of the soldiers hit the man on the back with the butt of his rifle.

The occupants of the building said he was clever and would find some way of getting out of gaol. Madame Laure trembled, and my aunt thought of installing steel bolts, thick ones, one on the upper part of the door and the other at the bottom. She was amazed at how a man of his size could have done it. When she talked about him later, she never failed to mention in practically every sentence how short and slender he was.

When they found Mathilde's severed limbs on the waste ground nearby, Madame Khayyat nearly fainted, like a ladder swaying on a floor. The children found other body parts buried on another piece of waste ground. When Madame Khayyat came out of her swoon, she said that she had heard

Mathilde's voice calling for help but did not believe what she heard. Mathilde had screamed twice, then made no further sound. Later, Madame Khayyat said that she had assumed they were quarrelling; that was why she went on watching the soap opera she followed on television.

My aunt was alone in the building. No one stood at the large windows that lighted the stairs and separated the floors. No one opened their door. From Mathilde's abandoned doorway one could see the frame of the bed, which the explosion had thrown to the end of the long hall. It was antique, and damaged in several places. One could also see, from where the door had been ripped off, a leg and corner of the table, old and worn out. The debris from Mathilde's flat still lay there. It filled the hallway and some of the living room, and had wrecked the door of the Arab-style bathroom.

Madame Laure had grown used to Mathilde's flat and no longer feared it. She stood beside her husband as he picked up one of the door panels in order to reposition it and seal it. He placed wooden planks across the door and nailed them securely. Madame Laure never left his side. She watched his broad forearms as he lifted the heavy door panel. He rolled up his shirtsleeves. In the wide vacant lot, after the explosion, he puffed out his chest and pumped up his arms, the way young taxi drivers do. The tenants met there. The man who had lived in the watchman's house set out chairs for them, in the shade. They showed up one by one. My aunt's husband was angry, his brows knitted. Some of his hairs had turned white, and his forehead seemed higher beneath his receding hair. Like Abraham, he kept his arms pulled aggressively away from his body. When he sat on the chair, one could see a gap in his mouth, in the space where two or three teeth should have been.

My aunt was alone in the building. Everyone else had left. She said no one was left but Ahmad al-Siblini's family – they would come in a few days and take away the rest of the furniture. Madame Laure had left, and the man on the second floor had great difficulty getting out what remained of his un-damaged furniture. The al-Kilanis had not come back to their flat after the explosion. The freckles on Umm Ibrahim's shoulders could be seen over the rest of her cool, tender skin: she was not aware of her nakedness in front of the crowds of people down below when the fireman hoisted her over his shoulder and carried her down the long metal ladder. On the ground, the two other firemen shone a beam of light on her, the fireman, and the balcony railing. The crowds of people assumed she was unconscious as she lay thrown over his shoulder, and still thought so after she placed one foot on the ground. She looked haggard, her eyes staring up at the balcony of her flat.

She did not gather with the rest of them in the vacant lot. They were all men, and seemed as if they were looking for someone to help them, and yet at the same time all of them made a point of moving and gesturing in a way that suggested how strong they were. The man from the watchman's house brought them coffee. They did not ask his opinion. He stood among the chairs but said nothing. They agreed that it had been the landlord – he had planted explosives, because the explosion had happened two hours after the latest ceasefire. Ahmad al-Siblini said that he knew an excellent lawyer. The man from the second floor said he knew another lawyer, who was a relative of his. They passed around a sheet of paper with a few lines of petition written at the top. They agreed on the wording, and signed it. They laughed a little about this, and then got angry. Al-Siblini said that he would volunteer to go and meet the landlord, with one other person. Abraham stood up. Every so often another person came through the iron gate and into the empty lot; they would watch him as he drew closer from where they sat in the shade. Then he would be among them, shaking hands with each of them one by one, congratulating them on their safety.

My aunt was alone in the building. The interior of her flat had not changed, and she still watered the plants in the tin pots that she had lined up along the sides and front of the big balcony. The building was empty except for her flat. It looked like the abandoned suite of an old beach hotel. She would no longer hear the sound of the frying pan suddenly sizzling on the flame and then dying down. She would no longer see her clean kitchen apron. She said she had waited a long time before she was able to come back up to the flat. The façade of the building was smashed and had subsided. The two little gardens under the Russian lady's window and the window of the neighbouring flat had been torn up when the entrance to the building was extended a little. Now it was colourless concrete, and seemed to lean to one side, like a man standing on one foot.

The occupants had all helped to build the steps and renovate the entrance to the building. It cost them less than they expected. They changed nothing in the wrecked flats on the second floor; in fact they left them empty, so they put up two tall supporting columns that reached from the ground floor up to the entrance of those two flats. The columns were in the middle of the hall inside the entrance of the building. The occupants wondered what good they were, since the staircase stood without them. The al-Kilani flat was still defaced by the handprints and childish drawings on the walls. The towel had fallen from the metal ring in the other flat.

It was as if they had built the steps solely for my aunt's use. They installed a new railing of unpainted iron along the stairs of the first three storeys. The bare cement of the steps and the iron railing made the building seem stronger and more solid than it really was.

The landlord waited for them to finish the stairs and the entrance and met them one by one. In their first negotiation, they asked impossible sums in exchange for their departure. They met together again, and as they were talking, they heard that Umm Ibrahim al-Kilani had agreed to leave. She had left her flat, and so had the man from the other apartment on the second floor; he agreed a short time later. The landlord dealt with them one by one, all except my aunt, who remained alone in the building, high on the fifth floor, as if it were an old beach hotel.

She would accept only the amount she had been demanding from the beginning. The lawyer told her that there was nothing the landlord could do. He was young and earnest, and devoted all his time to this one case. He brought her news of its progress little by little. Sometimes she saw him on the stairs and sometimes at the entrance to the building, and more often in the al-Munla district. It was his first case; that was why he put so much effort and labour into it and that was why my aunt was so certain he would lose it.